I had helped develop the thing, and there were some people who couldn't forget it, and who weren't about to forgive me my part in it.

The chain reaction worked for a hundred square miles before it wore itself out. Then a helicopter went in to check. To a depth of three feet the area had been transformed to slick, hard, brown volcanic glass. It was still smoking. Here and there a bubble. No sign of the observation team, the blockhouse. No trees, no grass, no rocks. Just this hard, shiny, smoking stuff, clear to the horizon. Just a hundred square miles of the face of the earth fused to nothing.

It would make quite a weapon, if we'd learned how to control it. Men had given their lives to prove it. Whatever it was, it was going to get itself discovered whether the human race was ready for it or not.

Nina Rasmussen was one of those people who weren't ready, who wouldn't accept things as they were, who didn't forgive or forget. She was a dis-arming creature. You might have thought of her as the girl next door, until you got to know her . . .
I got to know her.

Assassins Have Starry Eyes

FORMER TITLE—ASSIGNMENT: MURDER

by Donald Hamilton

A Gold Medal Book

GOLD MEDAL BOOKS
Fawcett Publications, Inc., Greenwich, Conn.
Member of American Book Publishers Council, Inc.

ONE

I GOT UP at five forty-five, started the stove, and went down to the creek for water. I had to crack ice to get it. The kids in the camp above me already had a big fire going. I envied them; a gasoline stove is convenient, but it doesn't keep your fingers warm while you're cooking breakfast. Of course, there was no law against my building a fire too. The bacon was hard as plywood, and the eggs were frozen in their shells and fell into the pan like blobs of jello. A middle-aged man from the small trailer parked below me came by on his way back from the john and shivered in an exaggerated way as he passed, grinned, and paused to speak.

"If the Army had ordered us here we'd be griping our heads off. Ain't it hell what people will do for fun and venison? All by yourself? Come on down, the wife's making breakfast."

I said, "Thanks, but I've already got this started."

"Well, good luck."

"The same to you," I said, sitting down on a log to eat out of the frying pan. I don't know why it is a man camping alone will always cut all the corners he can. Last year, 1954, I recalled, we had Jack Bates's big wall tent and Larry DeVry's folding table and chairs; and even on opening day breakfast had come up with fruit juice, hot rolls, and all the trimmings. Well, this morning Jack and Larry were luxuriating down in the Mogollon country somewhere, with a couple of other guys from the Project, and I was sleeping on the ground up here and eating off my lap.

They would be on their second cup of coffee by now, I reflected, and they would be talking the usual mixture of guns and game, sex, physics, politics and security, with maybe a few fishing reminiscences thrown in despite the season. There would undoubtedly be some sympathetic reference to poor Greg who was taking it pretty hard, and a moment of respectful silence for another man's marital difficulties.

. . . I grimaced, rose, dumped some water into the skillet and left it to soak, and went over to roll up my sleeping bag and throw the ground-cloth over it in case it should rain—not likely at this time of year.

The two kids from above came by in their beat-up jeep, and waved as they went past. "Good luck, Mac," the nearest one shouted.

"Leave a big one for me," I called back.

Off in the distance somebody fired a gun. I glanced at my watch and made it illegal. Official daylight wasn't for twenty minutes yet. I had another cup of coffee. The deer could wait. I had no intention of entering the timber, even in the car, until it was light enough for people to see what they were shooting at. You get some wild men in the woods at this time of year.

I watched the sky get pale over the ridge beyond the creek. The mountain pines made a saw-toothed black silhouette, quite detailless as yet. Los Alamos would be over that way, I reflected. Nowadays you couldn't take two steps across New Mexico without falling over an atomic genius. Well, I was hardly in a position to complain about that, and the work had to be done somewhere—although since the accident to those Jap fishermen off Bikini and the publicity given last year's tests out in Nevada by the fallout-conscious press, our profession probably didn't seem quite as glamorous and romantic to the local populace as it had when nobody quite knew what the hell we were doing.

But anyway the sky was clear and it was going to be a fine day. There are a great many criticisms that can be made about this part of the United States, and I had heard most of them in the three years I had been married; but except for a little dust now and then nobody can find much fault with the climate.

I got into the car at last, drove out of the camp ground, turned right, headed up the gravel road for a mile, and turned right again up an old logging road I had spotted the afternoon before. It was rough going and didn't do the Pontiac a bit of good, but I had never liked that blue-and-cream creation, anyway. Like all the new cars, it looked like something to be kept under glass in a lady's bedroom, and since when am I too helpless to shift my own gears?

A mile and three-tenths from the gravel—I always log the distance when heading into unknown territory, in case I might have to walk out—there was a wooden bridge that looked doubtful, and nothing to be gained by taking a chance on it. I backed the convertible into the bushes and swung it around; if I was going to get stuck doing it, it might as well be now while I was fresh and had food in me. But I got around all right, although why they build cars twenty feet long will always be a mystery to me. There was pale daylight all through the woods now and sunlight on top of the mountains but not down where I was. I peeled off my sweater, exchanged my wool helmet for a red cap, and got the gun out of its case.

There's always something special, like a ritual, about loading a gun for the first time of the season—not that I hadn't fired a couple of boxes of shells through it during the past couple of weeks to zero it in and get the feel of it back. But this was for keeps, and I cleaned off the scope lenses, pulled the bolt and sighted through the bore to make sure it was clear, replaced the bolt, pressed five shells into the magazine, fed one into the chamber, and set the safety.

"Okay, deer," I said. "Here I come, ready or not."

With two apples, one Hershey bar, and half a dozen extra shells in my pocket, and the gun in my hand, I crossed the half-rotten bridge and started up the logging road at an easy pace. There's a theory to the effect that a man walking naturally won't scare game half as much as one sneaking along trying to make like Hiawatha; the deer figure the first guy is going on about his business, while the second is obviously up to no good. However that may be, there were too many dry leaves around for me to move quietly, so I just walked, keeping my eyes open for a suitable place to sit. In my experience, you'll see twice as many deer sitting still as you will loping across country, particularly when the woods are already full of fiddlefooted hunters who can be counted on to keep the game moving.

After a mile or so I found a nice stand. There was a long open expanse of slope to watch, as well as several hundred yards of the road winding on down the side of the ridge over which I had just come; and, very important, there was a dry stump to sit on. Nothing dissipates the joy of hunting as quickly as a wet tail. I climbed up there, looked the situation over, ate an apple, and just sat. The view, as always in that country, was terrific. I could look over the tops of the nearer trees and see the canyon open up to the west, finally merging with the desert country out there, just touched by the sun. The horizon was at least twenty miles away in that direction, probably nearer forty; and once past the main highway you could walk all day and find no sign of civilization except maybe a uranium prospector's jeep-track.

I can never comprehend how anyone can look at a view like that and not like it; but I have good reason to know that it depresses some people to encounter a lot of land on which nothing much grows. I saw this country first on a business visit to Alamos during the war; and I told myself at the time I was coming back. Now that I've lived out here for a while, it makes me nervous to go east and see green stuff sprouting all over the landscape. I have come to like a country that gives elbow-room to everybody and everything, even a blade of grass.

I tossed my apple core away, checked the gun, and sat some more. The wind, what there was of it, was in the right direction—toward me—but nothing seemed to be moving in the neighborhood except a couple of mountain jays. Once I raised the gun very slowly and used the four-power scope to examine a dead limb that might have been an antler but wasn't; then I put the weapon back on my knees. There was plenty of time. I was in no hurry. If I got my deer today, I'd have to head right back to Albuquerque to get it to the freezer plant before it spoiled. I'd just as soon take a few days. I expected to get one—I had filled my license every season so far—but I didn't want it to come too easy. There was nothing to go home for anyway.

It's very difficult to explain to a non-hunter why a normal and presumably sane man will drive a hundred and fifty miles over bad roads, sleep on the ground with the weather below freezing, beat up his car and strain his lungs at eight thousand feet above sea level, just so he can sit on a stump waiting to shoot an animal that never did him any harm. It certainly isn't the meat alone, although I'll eat venison in preference to beef any day in the week. And it isn't entirely the fact that I've been hunting since I was big enough to carry a gun and see no reason to stop now, although that's part of it, too.

I guess it's largely a matter of proving to yourself that you can do it. We've got so far from fundamentals these days—driving down concrete super-highways in our blue-and-cream convertibles with hydramatic drive—that every now and then we've got to get out and prove to ourselves that we've still got feet and hands and eyes; and brains good for something besides turning out fancy equations for the electronic computers. We can, by God, climb a mountain and outwit a mule deer once a year. . . .

The bullet hit me in the back, to the left of the spine. Everything was very clear and lucid and I knew that I had been shot even before I heard the report behind me. Then I was on the ground on top of my rifle. I was in no particular pain, although I did seem to be a little behind in my breathing. I was mad and scared—very scared—and I yelled something, God only knows what. Something hit the stump on which I had been sitting a solid blow. People don't realize the power of modern firearms; this bullet went clear through the eighteen-inch stump, ripping out a fistful of rotten wood on the exit side.

"For Christ's sake, you crazy damn fool!" I shouted as loudly as I could manage; and I pulled off my red cap and, lying there, waved it as high as I could reach. A line of fire seemed to run across my arm. I snatched it back and looked at the torn sleeve and the blood beginning to ooze from the shallow burn. Another bullet smashed through the bushes beside me, hit the hillside, and went screaming off into space.

I tried to move—cautiously, because I expected it to hurt. There was no pain, but the wires were down. I had no control over my legs at all. I wondered if I were dying, and, more scared than ever, got my elbows under me and managed to wriggle off the gun, swing it around, and shove it out ahead of me, parting the thin oak brush into which I had fallen.

I can't recall making the decision. It kind of made itself, helped along by a faceful of dirt thrown up by the next bullet. Then I had him in the scope. He was standing in the thick bushes at the edge of the woods; all I could see was his head—with one of those luminous red hunting caps on it—and the carbine with which he was blazing away just as fast as he could pump the lever. The undergrowth made it difficult to see much of his body. As I say, I don't remember taking much time over the decision. I shot for the head. The recoil of the .270, which had never bothered me before, seemed to tear me apart inside, and I passed out.

TWO

I AWOKE TO full consciousness at last in a Santa Fe hospital, hooked up to what seemed like enough laboratory equipment to give Frankenstein's monster a good start in life. They had fitted me with exterior plumbing to use while my own system was undergoing repairs. I had a beard and a fancy assortment of tormented memories; and an uneasy feeling that people were going to want to talk to me, now that I could talk back. I was right about that.

The first one in was a stocky, dark, western character in a blue uniform. Despite the uniform, the badge and gun, you would never for a moment have mistaken him for a Chicago or New York cop. The nurse who ushered him in told me that this was Sergeant Ramon Sagrado of the state police, who had stopped by to see how I was getting along. Having encountered the state police in their official capacity once before on a matter of speeding—I wasn't driving the car at the time—I happened to know that on the New Mexico force, sergeant ranks just below captain and above two different grades of patrolman.

Sergeant Sagrado asked a few innocuous questions, the nurse called time on him, and he departed, having let slip no more information than that I had killed a man—something of which I was already aware. I'm not quite the world's best marksman, but at seventy yards, with a scope, from the prone position, it's hard to miss; and I had used my .270 often enough on game to have a fairly good, if unpleasant, idea of what it would do to a man's head. I had not yet decided how I was going to feel about it, however, and did not do so now. It was easier just to go back to sleep.

The following afternoon, Van Horn dropped in to see me. "Well, Dr. Gregory," he said, "you *will* go hunting, no matter what anybody tells you."

"Yep," I whispered.

"Now, if you'd hurt yourself in an automobile accident

10

or ruptured your appendix," he said, pulling up a chair, "I'd be full of sympathy and concern. But any man who's fool enough to go out into a forest full of other men with guns—particularly a man in your position—deserves anything he gets. Not to mention the fact that I fail to see what pleasure anybody can find in using a high-powered rifle to annihilate an inoffensive deer."

"It's a mystery," I agreed in my weak whisper, "like why anybody would put twenty pounds of old iron on a little wheeled cart and drag it three or four miles through a cow pasture under the hot sun just to beat at a harmless little white ball—"

"Well, at least I never wound up in the hospital from it," he said, taking out his pipe and scratching the bowl with a small-bladed penknife.

He was just an average-looking guy, not short not tall, not fat not thin, about forty or a little over, in a brownish suit, a light topcoat, and a light Stetson with a medium wide brim that he had bought after coming out here and referred to as his disguise—apparently his previous work with the F.B.I. had not often sent him west of the Mississippi. Nobody quite knew whether he was still with the Bureau and just out on loan, so to speak; or whether he had actually quit to take the job with the Project. He had the title of Chief of Security. Rumor said that while with the F.B.I. he had killed four men in the line of duty. He didn't look it. Well, I had killed one and I hoped I didn't look it either.

"Well," he said in a resigned voice, "tell me what happened."

"The guy shot me," I whispered. "He kept on shooting. It seemed likely that if he worked at it long enough he would hit me again, so I shot back."

"Uh-huh," he said, stuffing tobacco into his pipe. "Hit him in the left eye and cracked his skull like a ripe melon. Not bad for an amateur."

"I'm so glad you approve," I whispered. "And I do thank you for the graphic description."

He said calmly, "If you were going to be sensitive about it, the time to start was before you pulled the trigger. As a matter of fact, you have reason to congratulate yourself on your marksmanship. Since the other fellow obviously did no shooting after he was hit, there's no doubt in anyone's mind that he must have fired his five shots at you before you shot back, which, taken with your wound, makes a clear case of justifiable homicide. Normally there's a public hearing in any case involving homicide, justifiable or otherwise, but under the circumstances, after some discussion with Washington, the local authorities have agreed to drop the matter. So you can quit holding your breath now."

I whispered, "I don't like that. It smells like a cover-up. If there's supposed to be a hearing, I want a hearing."

He grinned. "What you want, Dr. Gregory," he said gently, "is one of the lesser problems confronting the administration in Washington. They, for obvious reasons, want no unnecessary publicity. The case is therefore closed. Now tell me: was he shooting at a deer or a man?"

I glanced at him. He was lighting the pipe now. "I assumed a deer," I said.

"Why?"

"No reason to think otherwise."

"None except the striking coincidence of a key research man getting shot shortly after completing his report on the initial phase of a very hush program from which great things are expected."

I said, "If I'd been shot before completing the report, it would have been even more striking."

"You were wearing a red cap and a red plaid shirt, and sitting on a stump in the middle of an open clearing. How in God's name could anybody have mistaken you for a deer? Enough to fire five shots at you?"

I said, "It may sound screwy, but it happens every year. It was the morning of the first day of the season. The guy was keyed up; he snapped a shot at something he just saw out of the corner of his eye. The target flopped and started crashing around in the brush. As far as he was concerned, the biggest damn buck in the world was down over there, and was he going to let it get away? Not on your life."

He said, "If you're so sure of that, why did you shoot to kill?"

"What do you mean?"

"If you'd shot for the body, he might have stood a chance."

I whispered, "He was standing in brush up to his neck. A .270 won't shoot through brush, not with the 130-grain load I was using. The bullet's too light, traveling too fast. Any little twig will deflect it or even make it fly apart. I should tell you about bullets? I shot at the only target I stood a reasonable chance of hitting, Van. Don't build any fancy theories on that. At the time, I never thought that it was anything but a trigger-happy hunter."

"And now?"

"I still think so. If somebody wanted me dead, they'd have sent a better shot. Or a guy who could at least keep his head when he missed the first one. There I was, anchored to the spot, yelling at him to stop shooting, obviously suspecting not a thing. All he had to do, if murder was his business, was to come running up with an expression of shock and concern on his face, ask me how badly I was hurt, fuss around trying to make me comfortable, set my gun out of reach—and slit my throat from ear to ear. Instead of which he stood blazing away, just hoping if he fired enough shots in my general direction one would connect. Is that the behavior of a steel-nerved professional killer, or of an excited deer hunter?"

Van Horn grinned. "You make it sound very plausible. I can see you've given it some thought, which is kind of significant in itself. Well, we're checking. I might add that we're getting not a damn thing. So far. But there's the interesting coincidence of the young fellow and his hunting companion picking the same camp ground you had chosen; and I don't like coincidences—"

"Wait a minute!" I whispered. "Two kids in a jeep . . . One of those?"

"Didn't you know? His name was Hagen, Paul Hagen. His partner's name was Antonio Rasmussen—there's a nice New Mexico combination of names for you. We're checking on him too. They were both students at the University, which may or may not mean something." He glanced at his watch. "Well, I'd better get out before the nurse kicks me out. I've stuck a couple of men next door, just in case somebody might try again. Three rings on the buzzer will get them. Take it easy."

I watched him leave. The door closed. I relaxed and closed my eyes, suddenly very tired. Into my mind, unbidden, came a picture of the two youngsters riding by in their battered jeep. One of them had wished me luck and both had waved, I remembered. There are probably few hunters who, watching the odd specimens who head into the woods with guns each fall, haven't said to themselves: *If some trigger-happy moron opens up on me, he'd better not miss, because I won't.* But having the thought is a little different from acting on it. . . .

When I opened my eyes again, she was standing there, holding the door open to show that she was prepared to leave if she was not welcome. She was wearing the mink coat she had had when we were married and the small hat she had bought on her last trip back east.

"Hi, Princess," I whispered. "How was Reno?"

THREE

SHE LET THE door swing closed under its own power and came forward. I noticed belatedly that she was carrying an armload of flowers wrapped in tissue paper—it was difficult to see how I could have overlooked it, since the package was almost three feet long. Perhaps I had been thinking of other things than flowers.

"Ring for the nurse, will you, darling?" she said. "So I can get rid of this stuff. My God, they've really got you wired for sound."

I found the buzzer and pressed it, saying, "They're planning to fit me with the proper connections so that when I get home I can just shove the laundromat to one side and hook myself up to the Albuquerque water and sewage systems. Make a fine husband for some woman. She can plug me in the wall socket when she wants my company; switch me off and roll me back in the corner when she doesn't. A great improvement over the old-fashioned kind of husband that's always taking off for the office or duck blind or what have you." A young nurse's aide put her head in the door. I whispered, "Bring a bathtub or something, will you, please? We've got flowers."

There followed the usual confusion that seems to be inevitable when a couple of females get involved with a bunch of flowers. They tried three different pots before the girl found a glass pitcher deep enough to hold Natalie's contribution, and then they had to get the bouquet organized. The flowers were gladioli, of that red-orange shade that went nicely with the light-green living room walls back home. I told myself the color had no particular significance, although it was the color I had usually tried for when I figured we had fought long enough and it was time to quit.

Finally Natalie thanked the girl, saw her out the door, and turned to look at me again. "You don't have to start right out being unpleasant," she said. "You might appreciate me first, just for a minute or two. I've driven eight hundred miles since yesterday morning to get here."

I shuddered at the thought. She had the quaint idea that a car was barely moving until the needle registered eighty. "Who's being unpleasant?" I whispered.

"I didn't like that crack about husbands and laundromats and other conveniences."

"Sorry," I whispered. "Meant to be funny. Consider it withdrawn. Thanks for the flowers."

She remained by the door for a moment longer; a slight girl, no taller than average but somewhat straighter, with dark hair that she still wore quite long despite the current whacked-off styles. With her big eyes and big red mouth, the shoulder-length dark hair gave her the look of a prematurely sophisticated schoolgirl. She had been twenty when I married her; she was twenty-three now. The whole thing had been a mistake, of course, but I could still think of arguments in its favor.

She made a little gesture that covered the bed, the apparatus, and me. "How bad?" she asked.

"Think nothing of it. I can wiggle my toes and everything."

"The paper said you were in a critical condition. It was last Sunday's *Albuquerque Journal* somebody'd left in the hotel lobby; I was looking through it at breakfast just for old times' sake. I expected to get here just in time to hear your last words."

I whispered, "I've always been a disappointment to you, haven't I, Natalie?"

"Go to hell," she said, and grinned. "You certainly are a helpless-looking character in that bed."

Then the grin faded, and she turned abruptly away to remove her hat and pick up the purse she had laid aside while messing with the flowers. I could see her both front and rear as she stood before the dresser mirror lighting a cigarette; her eyes were tired, but her navy-blue dress was fresh. She had obviously taken time to shower and change somewhere before hastening to my deathbed. I suppose any woman would.

She said, "I suppose it's all right to smoke."

"Sure," I said. "But this kind of louses up your legal residence requirements, doesn't it? I thought you weren't supposed to leave Nevada for six weeks, or something."

She said, "That's gratitude for you. I practically kill my-

self to get here, and the man quotes the law at me." She
swung back to face me. "Aren't you just a little bit glad
to see me, darling?"

"I'm always glad to see you, darling," I whispered.
"Looking at you is the only thing that never ceased to be
a treat—well, almost the only thing. But when people leave
I kind of like them to stay left, if you know what I
mean. What are you trying to prove, Princess?"

She drew on her cigarette, looked at it, and blew smoke
at it. "What if I wanted to come back?"

I said, "I appreciate the thought, but you're not Florence
Nightingale. They're taking fine care of me here. The fact
that some damn fool shot a hole in me doesn't change the
situation at all, as far as I can see. If you couldn't stand
it before, what's going to make you stand it now?"

"What," she said, "if I told you how much I'd missed
you?"

I said, "It's sweet of you to say so, and I missed you,
too. So what? If you'd lived three years with a dog, you'd
miss it when it wasn't around any more."

"My God," she said, "you are a bastard, aren't you?"

"You've said so before."

"Here I drive across that damn desert a hundred miles
an hour with tears streaming down my face. . . ." She
grinned abruptly. That grin always looked misplaced on
her delicate face; it belonged on a tomboy. "Good old Greg.
You don't know what a relief it is to hear you talk like
that. If you'd been gentle and grateful I'd have known you
were dying. Do they let you kiss the patients in this in-
stitution?"

I whispered, "I don't know. Try it and see."

She leaned over the bed and touched her lips to mine
chastely. I recognized her perfume as something I had
given her, a local product called "Nightblooming Cereus,"
made from the desert flower.

She looked down at me. "You ought to do something
about those whiskers. Look, you *are* going to be all right,
aren't you? Greg, what the hell are we going to do?"

"I don't know," I said. "It's a complex situation."

"It's a very simple situation," she said. "If you weren't
such a louse, and had a halfway civilized job in a halfway
civilized place—"

I whispered, "New Mexico was settled while Massachusetts
was still a howling wilderness, not to mention your home

state of New York. And if there's a more civilized job than mine, I don't know what it is."

"Then God help civilization," she said and kissed me again lightly, and straightened up. "I don't suppose you can get a drink around here."

"No, I don't suppose so."

"And you couldn't drink with me, anyway."

"You might run over to La Fonda and bring back a pitcher of martinis," I whispered. "Take a sip yourself, and pour a slug into this equipment for me. I think the mouth is over there."

She laughed and stood looking at me for a moment; and said abruptly, "You *will* be all right, won't you, Greg?"

I said, "The doctor claims the works are all there, if that's what you mean. It may take a month or two to put them back together again, but that's all. Why? Do I look that bad?"

She shook her head. "It's not that. It's just—" She hesitated. "Maybe I just feel a little responsible. The minute I leave you, you wind up at death's door."

I said, "If you're even toying with the notion that I went out into the woods and shot myself because I was so depressed over losing you, you're crazy."

She laughed. "Now I know why I went away," she said. "It was because I knew you'd try so hard to make me feel good when I came back." She turned away, got into her coat, found her gloves and pulled them on. Putting on a pair of gloves seems to be one of the most sophisticated routines a woman can perform, and Natalie was not one to slight her audience. "Well, I'll see you tomorrow," she said when the show was over. "Having come this far, I might as well stick around to see how you make it. . . ."

She had started for the door, but she stopped as it opened. It opened just enough to let a girl slip through the crack sideways, and closed again. Natalie glanced at me quickly, a little surprised. I had never seen the girl before.

I watched her put her back against the nearest available piece of wall, as if afraid something might jump on her from behind. She was about five feet six, a sunburned girl with blond hair cut boyishly short to show her neck and ears. She was wearing a boy's shirt and one of those wide, yellow, pleated skirts that southwestern females have borrowed from the Indians. Why any girl would go out of her way to look like a squaw, I couldn't tell you. My visitor was bare-legged and wore moccasins on her feet. One of the peculiarities of the natives of the region is that only the men wear high heels.

The girl kept her shoulders against the wall and watched us warily—I should say that she watched me, since she had given no sign of being aware of Natalie's presence.

"Dr. Gregory?" she said. "Dr. James Gregory?"

I nodded. She licked her lips, which needed lipstick. What little she had was badly chewed. "I'm Nina Rasmussen," she said. "You don't know me, but I have a brother named Tony, and I used to have a fiancé named Paul Hagen but I don't any longer. Thanks to you, Dr. Gregory."

I started to speak, but thought better of it. There was, after all, nothing to say. The girl gripped her purse tightly, almost wringing it between her hands.

"Don't bother to say it, Dr. Gregory," she whispered. "It wasn't your fault, was it? You were just defending yourself, weren't you? Paul shot first. You can't help it if an irresponsible fool can't bother to distinguish between a man and a deer. So you put a bullet neatly through his head to teach him a lesson. You must be very proud of your marksmanship, Dr. Gregory! But if you're such a wonderful shot, why did you have to kill him? That's what I want to know, Dr. Gregory: why, why, *why?*"

It was obviously no time to discuss the ballistic properties of the Winchester .270 cartridges. I did not like the look in the girl's eyes. I moved my hand slightly. It was a mistake. The push button, at the end of its cord, was pinned to my pillow in plain sight. When my hand moved, Nina Rasmussen reached into her bag and brought out a .22 automatic pistol.

Then we all looked at the gun, which seemed suddenly to dominate the white room. Even the girl looked at it, as if a little startled to find herself holding it. It was the low-priced Hi-Standard model with four-and-a-half-inch barrel and fixed sights. It had been shot a lot by somebody, from the looks of it; and the steadiness of her hand indicated that Nina Rasmussen might have done some of the shooting. You can usually tell, with a pistol particularly, when they know something about it. I had a disturbing mental picture of this girl, her brother, and Paul Hagen innocently camping out in the woods and tossing tin cans into the creek to shoot at. . . .

"Miss Rasmussen—"

I did not know what I was going to say; and she did not allow me to finish. "I know why you did it," she breathed. "I know why you shot to kill, deliberately. Because you people think you can make your own laws. Don't you? You come out here and spoil our country and poison our air with your horrible experiments, and nobody's got a right to protest because you're supposed to represent scientific progress or something. And when a man fires a shot at you by mistake, you turn and calmly blast him out of existence. You're above the law, above justice, above mercy, above humanity. Well, you're not above death, Dr. Gregory!"

The gun steadied. I saw her thumb move the safety down. It was the second time in a week that I'd looked a gunbarrel in the eye; and just as at the first time, I could not quite believe that it was happening to me, even as I tried to roll myself aside and heard the sharp and nasty bark of the .22 cartridge, very loud in the small room. I could not seem to find any strength or leverage. Then I was still lying there unharmed; and Nina Rasmussen was pawing aside the navy-blue purse Natalie had thrown with force and accuracy to spoil her aim. The girl looked around in time to catch the big pitcher of gladioli alongside her head, and crumpled to the floor in a mess of water, broken glass, and red-orange flowers.

FOUR

ONCE IT WAS over, it developed some of the elements of comedy. Everything was pretty wet including Natalie herself; and there were gladioli all over the room. Drawn by the shot, Van Horn's men came charging with ready guns, and one of them slipped on the wet rubber tiles and did as pretty a sit-me-down as you could ask. After that, however, it became less funny, since the Rasmussen girl turned out to have concussion and a bad cut on her head. Blood in large quantities has a way of taking the humor out of any situation. In the midst of all the fuss something started to happen to me, and I felt myself go out and down, almost without warning.

It was damp and dark down there, and it hurt; they came down after me and hauled me back, but it took a while—several days, in fact. When I opened my eyes again to daylight, Natalie was sitting in the chair by the window, wearing her big horn-rimmed reading glasses and reading a book. There were lots of things to be said against the girl, but in her favor was the fact that she could and did read. Maybe it would have been better if she had spent her time in front of the television set. Being an egghead myself, in the modern terminology, I wouldn't have much missed a wife who entertained me at breakfast by telling how Lucille Ball made out the night before. Besides, she was always getting herself into a fine state of indignation at the affairs of the world. Nobody could run the planet for thirty seconds to suit her.

I watched her now for a while, reflecting that it was funny all the commotion people raised about love. There had never been much question about the fact that we loved each other, from the time we first met at an official cocktail party given by somebody important at the University of Chicago. That was while the Project was in its preliminary stages, before it had even been given a home of its own. I was in town seeing about getting Larry DeVry

21

to work with us—they were letting me pick my own team, as they called it—and she was in town with her father, who was being hit for money by some scientific foundation connected with the University, and had flown out from New York to see what he was being asked to buy.

I suppose most men and their wives sometimes reflect upon the random combination of circumstances that brought them together; and I guess our combination was as random as any. Larry and Ruth had to go to the function since the math department was involved; and I was staying with them as I always did when in town, so they dragged me along. If you know the University, all modern Gothic, you know what the building looked like. The shindig was in one of the big reception rooms downstairs. I was talking to some man from Columbia—I've forgotten his name and the subject of the conversation—when I saw her enter.

If you've met the average faculty wife, you'll have some notion of how conspicuous Natalie looked in that place. I wasn't the only man who noticed her, by any means; but the competition wasn't serious. Most of it was married, and the rest was dedicated to science. There's a race of eager young research men who simply can't believe that the whole world, pretty girls included, isn't just as fascinated by their chosen fields as they are. Personally, I like to leave the stuff in the lab when I'm not working on a specific problem; and when I am, I particularly dislike talking about it except to people who know what I'm talking about. Perhaps that's why I never was worth much as an instructor.

Anyway, a couple of these dedicated characters had her pinned in a corner when I made my approach; they were trying to explain to her some abstruse theories and effects they should probably not have been mentioning in public.

She sent one of them for a drink and the other for her purse, which she claimed to have left on a chair somewhere. Then she looked at me and said coolly, "You look almost human. I've had about all the isotopic increment of the reactor frequency I can stand. Let's get the hell out of here."

"Sure," I said. "but what about your purse?"

She showed it to me, concealed under the furs draped across her arm. She grinned her surprising, tomboyish grin. "Don't be a wedge."

I played up. "What's a wedge?"

"The simplest tool known to man. This room is full of

simple tools, and I don't care if they are loaded down with Phi Beta keys until they walk bowlegged." She looked at me for a moment longer. I noticed that her eyes were greenish brown, called hazel. "Come on," she said, taking my arm. "I'll buy you a drink at the nearest bar, if you'll promise not to split a single atom, not even a little one."

Three weeks later we were married; and three years later I was still in love with her, and I thought she was still in love with me; and what good did it do us if we couldn't manage to figure out a way of living together under the circumstances my job required? I watched her now as she turned the page, big-eyed and studious; and I wanted her back more than I cared to admit, but what the hell? I had my work to do; and you can't have everything.

She looked up quickly. "Well, it's about time you woke up," she said, removed the glasses and dropped them into her bag, and rose and went out of the room, returning with the nurse who asked me the usual silly questions and took the routine readings.

"You can say hello to your wife, but she'd better leave in five minutes," the nurse said. "She'll be back tomorrow, won't you, Mrs. Gregory? We don't want another relapse, do we?"

We waited until she was gone. "Hello," Natalie said.

"Hello," I whispered. "How long have you been sitting there?"

"A couple of days, off and on. I'm staying at the hotel. My God, what a bunch of men in this town! They're either so artsy-craftsy they'd turn your stomach, or they wear high heels and smell of cows, or they've been associating with uranium so long they glow in the dark. Half a dozen characters have tried to pick me up in the bar; and each one of them started out by bringing out a piece of rock and juggling it casually for a while and then shoving it quickly under my nose and saying, 'Lady, do you know what that is? That's pure horsematite; runs umpteen per cent uranium oxide!' "

I laughed. There was a funny kind of awkwardness between us. It's hard for two people to talk in a relaxed way when they don't know if they're going to stay married or not.

Natalie said, "Your homicidal girl friend's in a room downstairs, under observation. There's a policeman in front of the door. She seems to be doing all right. No skull fracture or anything. I asked."

"Have you heard what they're planning to do with her?"

"Well, there was some talk of preferring charges as soon as you are well enough to testify."

"Charges?" I whispered. "What charges? She was trying to sell me a secondhand gun, since I'm interested in guns. Some fool had left a shell in the chamber and it went off. The noise startled her so she slipped and knocked over a pot of flowers. Why, you saw the whole thing with your own eyes."

Natalie lit a cigarette, and blew smoke in my direction. "If that's the way you want it, darling."

"I had it coming," I whispered. "I shot her boy-friend. I'm not apologizing, under the circumstances, but the girl was right in a sense: I made a decision nobody's got a real right to make. The least I can do is accommodate myself to the fact that some people aren't going to like me for it, and not mess up their lives any more than I've already done. She's got it out of her system; it seems unlikely that she'll try again. Tell them to let her go, Princess. They won't get any testimony out of me."

Natalie watched me for a moment longer. I could not tell what she was thinking. She was wearing a gray-green cashmere sweater and a pleated plaid skirt that involved a good deal of the same color among several others. She looked like a college girl. The skirt rippled nicely when she moved. I'm a sucker for pleats. The sweater was a loose fit, and she put no severe strains on it; however, I have never understood the current fad for outsize bosoms. If I want milk I can always buy a cow.

She said, "For a cold-blooded scientific bastard, you're a surprisingly nice guy. Sometimes." She stepped forward and leaned down to kiss me, holding the cigarette aloft. "I can hardly taste the man for the whiskers," she said, smiling. "You look like Ernest Hemingway; you're even getting some gray in spots."

"Well, you know who put it there."

"I suppose I ought to be jealous. Would you turn me loose if I tried to shoot you?"

"Hell, no," I said. "You're dangerous."

"Don't underestimate that girl just because she's a blonde and doesn't know how to dress."

"Underestimate her?" I whispered. "You sound as if I

was planning a long and happy relationship with the kid."

"Kid, hell," Natalie said. "She's a couple of years older than I am. That robust type doesn't grow up before forty." She grinned her mischievous grin. "And how would I know what you're planning? Well, I guess my time's up. I'll see you in the morning."

Toward the end of the week it was decided that I was strong enough to have a little more work done on the interior; I spent the morning in surgery and had no visitors that day. The following day it started snowing and Natalie called up from Albuquerque where she had gone to pick up some clothes and stuff; she left a message with the nurse that the roads were too bad for her to make it back, which I could well believe, looking at the white stuff falling past the window. Our friends in the east seem to labor under the delusion that we live in a tropical climate; they forget that Albuquerque is five thousand feet in the air, and Santa Fe, seven thousand. You get some weird scenes around here in the winter, with all the desert country and its spiny vegetation covered with snow. There's nothing more unlikely-looking than a snow-covered cactus.

I lay in bed and tried not to feel neglected, and fell asleep doing it. A knock on the door awakened me.

"Come in," I said.

It was one of Van Horn's men. "Do you want to see a young fellow named Rasmussen, Dr. Gregory?"

"A fellow named Rasmussen? Not a girl?"

He shook his head. "Her brother. After the hassle last week the desk figured they'd better clear with us. Should I tell him to go roll his hoop?"

I said, "No, send him up. Without a gun."

"Don't worry. He'll be safe as a little white mouse."

He went out; a few minutes later there was another knock, and a boy came in. I would not have recognized him on the street, although I had seen him once before up in the mountains. If there was any resemblance to his sister at all, it was in the mouth and eyes. This was a slender dark youth with olive skin, wearing dark, pleated slacks, a pink sports shirt, and a straight light jacket with a zipper down the front, which was open. He stopped just inside the door.

"I didn't mean to panic the joint, Dr. Gregory," he said. "I just . . . I mean, Nina wanted me to thank you. For getting her released. She just blew her top there for a while. She's all right now. I mean, there won't be any more trouble."

I said, "How is she feeling?"

He grinned, showing very white teeth against his dark face. "Lousy. They shaved off half her hair. She won't be fit to live with till it grows out." His grin died. "I guess the whole thing was pretty much my fault, Dr. Gregory. I was . . . .well, when something like that happens to a friend of yours you like to blame it on somebody; and I guess I just shot my mouth off too much around the house. Don't pay any attention to anything she said in here; she was just quoting me and my big mouth. . . . I still can't figure it, Dr. Gregory. Paul taught me how to handle a gun; he was always bearing down on how you should be careful. Well, I guess it was just one of those things. Well, Nina just wanted me to thank you. I guess I'll be running along."

When he opened the door, I caught a glimpse of Van Horn's man waiting outside. I suppose I should have been grateful for the protection, but the fact is that being under surveillance, even for my own good, is something I never get used to. Besides, who's kidding whom? You know damn well that if I didn't have some things in my head considered of value to the country I could hire myself out as a duck in a shooting gallery and no voice would be raised in protest. This business of having my brain and its contents considered public property, and myself only a kind of unreliable and possibly subversive custodian, gets irritating in the long run.

It wasn't irritating enough to keep me awake, however; and I slept through the afternoon and evening except for the usual breaks imposed by the hospital routine. Some time in the night I awoke suddenly, aroused by a sound outside. It was dark in the room except for the glow through the frosted glass of the hall transom. Then I heard a kind of scuffle beyond the door; and abruptly the door swung open, letting light pour in. I saw two silhouettes, one kind of pulling at the other, and heard a nurse's voice:

"*Please,* Mrs. Gregory! Visiting hours are over. I assure you he's perfectly all right—"

"You'd say that if he was dead and buried!" Natalie's enunciation was not quite as clear as usual. "Everybody in a hospital always says everybody's all right. Even when they're dying. . . . Greg?"

"Yes," I said.

She pulled herself free and came running across the room, a little unsteadily. The light came on abruptly, and I saw that she was wearing slacks and her mink coat; her head was bare and her long hair was a little untidy. There was more color in her face than usual, from the cold outdoors and from whatever she had been drinking; she looked very pretty.

"Greg, are you okay?" she cried. "Darling, I had the most horrible feeling—"

I said, "That's nothing to the feeling you're going to have tomorrow morning, Princess."

She stopped beside me, and giggled suddenly. Then she went to her knees beside the bed, put her face against the covers, and began to cry. The nurse was still standing by the light switch, looking stern and disapproving. One of Van Horn's men was at the door; maybe the one I had seen that afternoon, maybe not. I never bother to learn their names or remember their faces.

I said to both of them, "Get the hell out of here."

They went. Natalie said in a muffled voice, "That's telling the old bitch." Then she cried a little more. I patted her head in a gingerly fashion. After a while she said, "That damn house just got on my nerves, darling. Nobody in it but me. I made up a pitcher of martinis for company. Then I started . . . started worrying. I called the hospital long distance and they said you were doing fine, just fine, in that damn insincere voice they use for reassuring the family and friends. . . . I had another drink and was sure you were dying and I couldn't stand it any longer and I threw my coat on and got in the car and came on up. Fellow at a gas station said I couldn't make it without chains, but they just think in terms of Detroit iron. They don't know what baby can do. . . . Well, here I am. Are you really all right?"

"Yes," I said. "I'm fine. Doing very well. Everybody's proud of me."

"Excuse me for being a damn fool," she said.

"I don't mind," I said. "I'm used to it."

She made a face at me, and we looked at each other for a while.

I said, "You're a screwball, Princess. You might have killed yourself."

She said, "Look, let's stop this horsing around, darling. Do you want me back?"

I said, "Getting divorced wasn't my idea."

"Is that all you're going to say?"

I said, "The hell with you, Princess. I did all my crawling last summer. If you want to come back, come back, but don't expect me to get on my knees and ask you."

She said, "You don't leave a girl much pride."

I said, "You've got enough."

She said, "Well, I'm coming back. Somebody's got to look after you. And it's going to work this time. I'm going to make it work. You'll see. I'm just going to love this lovely old country with its lovely old dust storms and its fascinating old men in dirty old blankets and its enchanting old mud ruins. . . . I think I'll become an authority on old ruins. I might as well, everybody else is. What the hell are you laughing at?"

"You're drunk, Princess," I said. "Go over to the hotel and sleep it off."

"There he goes," she said. "After pleading with me for hours to come back to him, he's trying to get rid of me already."

FIVE

THEY LET ME come home for Christmas. It was the first time in my life I had been glad to leave picturesque old Santa Fe for Albuquerque, which is a big, impersonal, modern city; and one it's hard to get very fond of. There's no visible reason for its existence except tourist courts; and you can't see what the hell a tourist would want with the place. Aside from a small plaza, known as Old Town, there are few historical attractions; the scenery is nothing out of the ordinary for that part of the country; and the much-advertised Rio Grande—the historians' Rio Del Norte—is a string of mudflats much of the year, since most of the water is drained off for irrigation from early spring to late fall.

Despite these handicaps, you have one of the largest cities in the southwest sprawling over a God-forsaken stretch of desert along the banks of the little river that mostly isn't there. The city is divided into two parts; there's the Valley, and the Heights. The Valley is the river bottom; outside the downtown business district, green stuff will grow there if you water it with reasonable regularity. The Heights is the barren upland, or mesa, in the shadow of the abrupt Sandia Mountains east of town, and nothing grows there unless you soak it down good each night to keep it from blowing away in the morning. The bluff that divides the two sections is not precipitous, but it is quite noticeable, and the climatic difference is such that all Albuquerque weather reports give temperature readings for both parts of town. Since the Valley was taken up by the first comers, who weren't so dumb, all the new developments, including ours, are on the Heights.

Our house was of the local, single-story, flat-room, cement-block, picture-window design, plastered to look vaguely like the native adobe. The resemblance was sketchy, since adobe forms soft outlines and rounded corners, while no amount of plaster will camouflage the rigid rectangularity

29

of the blocks. The lots in this development were somewhat larger than average, giving me plenty of opportunity
for healthful exercise with the lawn mower; the watering
system for the lawn was built in, with sprinkler heads peep-
ing through the grass every twenty feet or so, which made
watering the lawn easier than it might have been. Our house
was pastel blue; the one to the north was pale yellow; and
the one to the south, baby pink. Somebody once told me
that this represented authentic old-time southwestern atmosphere, but I looked it up and found that most early
writers comment explicitly on the drab and monotonous appearance of New Mexico towns of their time. They were
all one color, the color of adobe mud. Maybe this is an
improvement.

I had never quite managed to think of the place as
home. For one thing, I'd had nothing to do with picking
it out or paying for it; for another, it was too much machinery and too little house. I was brought up in a big
old Wisconsin farmhouse; to me, a home is three stories
high and has an attic full of junk you don't use, and a
cellar full of junk you use, and a great big old coal furn-
ace—if it has central heating at all; we lived without it
for years—that has to be fed by a shovel in the hands
of yours truly. To be able to get heat into the place without even striking a match, and wash the dishes merely by
turning a button, is convenient to be sure, but it seems a
little like cheating. So does the fact that the whole works
was given to us as a wedding present by Natalie's father.

"I know you want a plate glass mansion on a hill, Princess," Mr. Walsh said in presenting us with the deed, "and
this man of yours probably wants a shack out in the
woods. While you're arguing about it, you can live here.
Don't bother to tell me you don't like it; I had it picked
for its investment value, and you can sell it any time you
decide what you really want. Here's a check toward the
furniture; I'll let you choose that for yourself."

That was three years ago, and I guess you get kind of
used to a place in three years. Despite my reservations
about it, I found myself remarkably pleased to see it again.
Natalie's little red sports car was in the driveway; she had
driven ahead to get things ready. The ambulance boys wanted
to cart me inside on the stretcher. I told them I had been
making the perilous journey to the john for a couple of
weeks now; I could manage to stagger into my own house.

There was a Christmas wreath with a big red bow on the front door. Before I reached the door, it swung open, and Natalie came out on the step in a short, shiny bright green dress with an inadequate bodice and a skirt that took up a lot of room and rustled when she moved. These old-fashioned hoops and crinolines the girls have been getting themselves up in of late look remarkably silly shopping in the supermarket, but they do have a nice, impractical, festive look for special events. She had a red ribbon in her hair and looked very Christmasy indeed. She took me by the arm.

"Brace yourself, darling," she said out of the corner of her mouth. "It's a goddamn surprise party."

We stepped inside, and a lot of people jumped out of the corners with bells, ringing them madly and singing—you guessed it—"Jingle Bells." At least it seemed like a lot of people after my cloistered hospital existence. Once the din had subsided and I had been deposited in a long chair with a blanket over my legs, the number reduced itself to three: Ruth and Larry DeVry, and Jack Bates.

Somebody put a vegetable-juice cocktail into my hand to give me something to hang onto, and Ruth said, "I hope you don't mind, Greg. I think surprise parties are silly, and I know you're tired after your long ride, but the boys were bound they were going to welcome you home, and Natalie seemed to think it would be all right if we didn't stay too long."

"Sure," I said. "It's swell, Ruth."

"You will let us know the minute you get tired."

"Sure."

She said, "It *is* good to have you back. We'd have come up to see you in the hospital, only at first they wouldn't let us and then, well, you know how it is just before Christmas. . . ."

She went on into a Christmas-shopping story. Natalie, with a drink in her hand, was talking to Jack Bates in front of the fireplace, which did not look quite like the fireplaces of my youth. Modern design apparently requires that nothing be built to look like what it is. We have a waffle iron that's streamlined for an air speed of approximately four hundred miles per hour. Similarly, our fireplace dispenses with a mantelpiece and has its chimney masonry concealed by discreet paneling so that, surprise,

surprise, nothing but the fireplace opening itself peeks out
at the room from another innocent wall.

Ruth was still talking. She was a thin and fairly tall
girl, with straight brown hair cut in a bang across her forehead, and glasses that always had something fancy in the
way of rims—tonight's were striped gold and black. She
wasn't bad looking by a good deal, but she had been better
looking when I knew them in Chicago. I'm no authority on
feminine beauty, but I have observed that women who go
too long without having children often tend to get a kind
of intense and frustrated and dried-up look. Not that I was
in a position to criticize. Our house wasn't resounding to
the patter of tiny feet. Ruth was wearing a long skirt of
some heavy Indian weave in a yellow-and-black pattern and
a brief black jersey bodice. A tremendous necklace of Indian
silver occupied most of the space left bare; and there were
similar bracelets on both arms. I did not dare comment on
the stuff because she collected it, and I did not want to
hear about the charming old squaw at the picturesque old
pueblo who had sold it to her for only thirty per cent more
than she would have paid for it at Marshall Field's back
in Chicago.

Friendships are funny things. Once I had been good
friends with Ruth DeVry, as well as with Larry. In Chicago
I used to practically live in their little apartment near the
University. It seemed a long time ago. When I spoke of it
to Natalie, she wanted to know if Ruth and I had ever
exchanged kisses or other tokens of affection when Larry
wasn't around.

I said, "Keep it clean, Princess. They were just friends of
mine, that's all."

"But didn't you ever think of it?" she insisted.

I admitted that there might have been times in those
long-lost days when slender, intense, artistic Ruth DeVry
had seemed very attractive to a lonely bachelor; however,
as a gentleman and a friend of her husband's, I had concealed my feelings.

"That," said Natalie, "is what you think. Why do you
think she hates my guts?"

Well, that was Natalie's theory, and I didn't put much
stock in it. The fact remained that Ruth got on my nerves
nowadays; and I was glad when Natalie and Jack Bates
came over to join us.

"Hi, Boss," Jack said. "God, you look terrible."

"You don't look so good yourself," I said. "What's the matter, have the women been running you ragged?"

He was a big, blond guy in his late twenties who liked anything that took him outdoors—and apparently, although he did not talk about it, a few things that took him indoors, as well. Van Horn had taken me aside to caution me about this tendency of his several months ago. Nowadays it seems that a man can't have any privacy at all in government service; even his love life comes under the heading of security information. Jack and I had struck up a hunting acquaintance in a duck blind on the Potomac while I was working in Washington; and when I needed a man with his qualifications, I remembered him. After all, physicists are a dime a dozen, but a man who can drop a passing canvasback at fifty-five yards is a jewel to be treasured and cherished.

If this seems like an irresponsible way of filling an important post, all I can say is that Jack Bates had been a life-saver in the lab, steady and conscientious and dependable; which is more than could be said for Larry DeVry who, despite our long-standing friendship and his brilliant qualifications as a mathematician, had turned out to be a hell of a prima donna on the job. Granted that it had been a tough assignment for him to turn around and work under me here, after seeing me through to my degree at a time when he was already an instructor at Chicago; nevertheless there had been times when I could see no sense to the temperamental performance he had put on. Even tonight, instead of joining in the festivities, he was browsing through my collection of classical records in an absorbed way, although he knew what was on the shelf as well as I did.

He was a small, dark specimen with glasses, who lived in a kind of fog of abstract numbers. It was typical of both of them that Jack had sent me, by way of Natalie, several batches of outdoors magazines in the hospital. Larry had sent me a box of candy. Only Larry DeVry would have thought of sending chocolate creams to a man convalescing from multiple perforations of the guts.

The three of us were always referred to by visiting celebrities as my "team." In the Army, everybody is a team; and while we were not strictly speaking in the Army, we never got lonely for the sight of uniforms. As far as I'm concerned, this team business is a lot of bunk. I never did get anywhere in any sport that demanded co-operation with a lot of other men. I can overlook the comic aspects of a couple of guys trying to whale hell out of a little round ball, just for fun, on a golf course or tennis court; but when five or nine or eleven get together and make a religion of it, you can count me out for laughing.

But the way some of the visiting VIP's talked, we at the Project were playing important ball in two leagues at once. There was the intramural league, in which the competition was represented by Los Alamos and various lesser centers of research around the country. The winner at this level would earn the honor of representing the country in the big, intercollegiate matches, to be climaxed, I guess, by the annual homecoming game against Soviet U. Now, I may not take my responsibilities as a Man of Science quite as seriously as some of my colleagues would like, but I'm damned if I'm going to belittle this atomic rat-race by treating it as a sport. So you'll hear no more reference to "teams" from me.

Seeing the rest gathering around the guest of honor, Larry gave up sulking and came on over. "It's good to have you back, Greg," he said. "Maybe now we'll get some action out of Washington. They've been sitting on that last report long enough."

Ruth said, "Now, boys. No shop talk."

Jack said, "Say, Greg, did you hear about Louis Justin?"

Ruth said, "Jack, I don't really think Greg should be worried—"

"What about Louis Justin?" I asked.

Natalie, sitting on the arm of my chair, said, "Who *is* Louis Justin, anyway? Oh, I remember, that's the one who had us to dinner up at Alamos and fed us enchiladas made with his own little hands." She ran her fingers through my hair. "I'm glad you don't like to cook, darling. There's something queer about any man who messes around a kitchen."

I said, "What about Louis Justin?"

"He's disappeared," Jack said. "Vanished. Evaporated. It's very mysterious. Six million security men are tearing their hair out by the roots, one hair at a time. It takes longer that way. Meanwhile, no Justin."

"How did it happen?" I asked.

"He was a ski-bug, as you probably remember. I suppose it was the Swiss in him coming out. Any time there was snow up on the mountain, Louie would be out there try-

ing to break a leg. His record was pretty good; he managed
to average one simple fracture a winter, with a compound
thrown in every couple of years for good measure. Sprains
and torn ligaments don't count. Well, a week or so ago
there was finally enough snow up in the Sangre de Cristos,
and Justin headed up to the ski-run to try it out. He
strapped the boards on his feet, took off, and was never
seen again. Van Horn is having kittens, pink ones with
chartreuse spots. It's not really his baby—it belongs to the
boys up at Alamos—but he's checking this end and talking
darkly about Burgess and Maclean, with a little Fuchs on
the side."

Larry shook his head. "It's hard to believe. Of course,
Louis always was an odd sort of person—"

"Oh, bunk!" Jack said rudely. "Don't you go climbing on
the little red bandwagon, too. Justin just cracked up like
old Fischer, who dived into Chesapeake Bay last summer
and let his boat sail home without him. Only Justin didn't
crack quite far enough to kill himself. God knows there
are times I get sick of this business, too. It would be nice
to take a powder to some pleasant island where the natives
do nothing more unfriendly than cook and eat each other.
I say chalk up another victim to the guilt of Hiroshima.
Justin's probably a thousand miles away, happily selling
size-five shoes to ladies with size-nine feet."

Larry said, "Isn't that a rather weak theory? I can't
imagine a sensible man with sound scientific training just
throwing up his career because of a sentimental impulse—"

"You'd rather believe he's a communist? What's sensible
and scientific about that?" Jack demanded. "And what has
scientific training got to do with it, anyway? Scientists get
scared just like anybody else, don't they? I know several
people, some with sound scientific training and some without, who've got estimates on bomb shelters for their back
yards in the past few years. Some have even laid in stocks
of canned goods, just in case. And the only reason more
aren't doing it is that they feel it probably won't do any
good. . . . It reminds me of a song we used to sing in
college." He hummed the tune. *"I went to the rock to hide
my face, and the rock cried out: no hiding place, there's
no hiding place down here."*

Everybody was quiet for a second or two. It seemed
about time to break this up. I said, "Who's replacing Justin
at Los Alamos?"

Jack didn't move at once; then he looked at me in a bemused sort of way. "What? Oh, why, nobody, as yet. We're clearing with Strohmeier for the time being. Not that there's much to clear until we get the go-ahead from Washington."

Ruth stirred uneasily. "This conversation is getting too serious," she said, "and Greg's had enough of us, anyway. Larry dear, let's let them have their Christmas Eve in peace. Come on, Jack, you're having dinner with us, remember?"

It took them a while to get their wraps. I watched the three of them go out the door together, Ruth in the middle. It gave me an odd feeling of watching a movie I had seen before—Jack was spending as much time at their place nowadays as I used to do some years before. Well, it was none of my business. Natalie waved good-by to them, closed the door, and let her party face slip.

"My God," she said, "you certainly know a bunch of grim people, darling."

I said, "We can't all be scintillating."

She grinned abruptly. "I'm sorry. I'm supposed to be good, aren't I? Your friends are wonderful, darling, simply wonderful. I just adore them. Where the hell's my drink got to?" She found it and came over to perch on my chair. I put my arm around her. She leaned back comfortably against my shoulder and said lazily, "You're supposed to be in bed."

I said, "Is that a prescription or a proposition?"

"Don't talk big," she said. "You're not *that* well."

I sighed. "Unfortunately, you're right. I couldn't get excited over Jayne Mansfield tonight, let alone a skinny little thing like you."

"You'd better be careful. You might hurt my feelings. Who was Fischer, darling?"

"I've told you about him. I worked with him in Washington for a while, setting up the Project. That was before I met you."

"What happened to him?"

"You heard what Jack said. He committed suicide off a sailboat six or seven months ago."

"And then you get shot. And then Louis Justin disappears. All people connected with the Project."

I said, "Old Dr. Fischer had been growing a conscience for years. Any time you tried to get sense out of him you'd first have to listen to his deep thoughts about the moral aspects of what we were doing. Weren't we usurping powers God had intended to reserve for himself? That routine. Personally, I figure that God's big enough to keep His secrets secret as long as He wants to. But it's a common disease in the profession. Even Jack's got a mild case; you heard him tonight wanting to slip away to a peaceful tropical island where nobody ever heard of an atom. Fischer had it bad. I wasn't too surprised when I heard what had happened."

Natalie glanced at me oddly. "You don't give the poor guy much sympathy, considering that you worked with him."

I said, "Princess, when a bunch of guys all have to face up to the same question, there's not going to be much sympathy for the man who cracks. He just makes it that much tougher for the rest. I get pretty damn tired of these spare-time philosophers of doom. Nobody ever invented anything important yet, in any field, that didn't create problems in other fields. The universities are lousy with social scientists; Washington is lousy with politicians. It's their problem; let them solve it."

"And what," she asked quietly, "if they can't?"

"Then," I said, "it's just going to be very, very tough, that's all. And the human race will suffer a setback of unpredictable dimensions because the so-called experts in human relations were too damn busy bickering about their childish political theories to keep up with the concrete facts handed them by us experts in physical relations. And I'm not going to fall off a sailboat because I did my job better than some other guys did theirs."

Natalie laughed. "That's what I love about you, darling, your humble and modest attitude." She drained her drink, set it aside, got up, and pulled the blanket off me. "Time for bed," she said. "I promised Dr. Barnett I'd look after you."

I got up. "Is that a new dress?" I asked.

"Uh-huh. Corny, isn't it? You can't buy anything but teen-age junk in this town." She grinned. "I mean, isn't it a darling little number; they have the most wonderful selection of clothes in this marvelous town. . . ." Her voice trailed off. She looked at me for a moment. "Damn it, it's nice to see you standing on your feet, you big bum," she said. "You know, you don't have to rape a girl to show affection. Just a kiss will do—for the time being."

SIX

I SPENT MOST of the winter practicing the tricks of digesting simple food and walking around the house. Never having been wounded or critically operated on before, I was surprised how long it took for my strength to return. Finally I was promoted to a less restricted diet and permitted to stroll around the neighborhood and ride in the car with Natalie to the local shopping center and even, presently, downtown. Even this adventure palled after a while, and I started yearning for some work to do—an unusual condition for me. Unlike many of my colleagues, who live and breathe only for their research, I have never really been sold on the merits of hard work. I can take the stuff or leave it alone. But in my weakened condition there was nothing more interesting to do.

However, I was caught in a tug-of-war between Dr. Barnett, who wouldn't hear of my setting foot on the Project before the first of April, and Van Horn, who wouldn't consider relaxing his regulations enough to let me work at home. He said that electronic eavesdropping devices had been perfected to such extent that he would not be able to guarantee security short of tearing down the place and building it over again. So I spent the time cleaning my guns—the police had returned the .270 badly finger-marked but fortunately nothing rusts in that dry climate—and overhauling my camping gear, reading books and listening to records, and having Natalie drive me out for fresh air whenever the house started driving me completely nuts.

One pleasant afternoon she talked me into using her little car for one of these excursions. Before she got it—as a gesture of independence the day before setting off for Reno —I thought I had this sports car business licked. The little ones were MG's and the big ones were Jaguars. Now I had to start all over again. This was something called a Triumph, of British manufacture. With the top down, it stood about knee high; it was fire-engine red; and it had ninety horsepower distributed among four cylinders, an eighty-eight-inch wheelbase, a thirty-two-foot turning circle, and a weight of about eighteen hundred pounds stripped and dry. I knew all about it because she left the descriptive brochure on the living room table the day she left me. The vehicle was capable of a hundred and twenty-four miles per hour in racing trim. The pamphlet didn't say why anybody would want to go that fast.

"The top is called the hood," she said as we went into the garage. "But it's too nice out to put it up today. The hood is called the bonnet. The trunk is called the boot. It runs on petrol and you spell the tires with a 'y.' Get in and hang on. . . . Not like that," she said as I stuck half way. "Don't try to walk into it. First sit down on the seat, then pull your legs up and swing them inside."

I followed instructions while she took a bright silk scarf from the pocket of her coat and tied it over her hair; then she got in beside me. It was quite a ride. In theory I disapprove of any piece of machinery designed wholly for speed on the highway, but the thing was obviously fun to drive and she looked cute driving it. We came back after dark, well wind-blown, to find the phone ringing. Natalie went across the room, pulling the scarf off her hair, to get it while I was closing the front door. She stuck her head back a moment later, saying:

"It's Larry. He says he's been trying to reach you for an hour. He . . . they want you at the Project right away. I told him it was against Dr. Barnett's orders, but he says it's an emergency."

I said, "Okay. Give me the keys of the Pontiac and tell them to clear the car through the gate so I don't have to walk from the parking lot." Normally, only official vehicles are allowed on the Project.

She said, "At least let me drive you."

I shook my head. "It's easier this way. Van Horn wouldn't let his own mother on the place without getting official clearance. which takes about six months. This way I can drive right up to the door." I grinned. "Hell, that glamor-buggy practically drives itself. I'm a big boy now, Princess; I'll be okay. Tell them I'm on my way."

To get to the Project, you go a certain distance out of Albuquerque in a certain direction. Presently you come to a stretch of desert fenced in like most of the country around here with an ordinary four-strand barbed-wire fence. Like practically all fences in the southwest—destroying any illusions you may have entertained about western hospitality —this one is liberally hung with unfriendly signs: NO TRESPASSING, NO HUNTING, NO WOOD HAULING. I think that if Mount Everest were located in this portion of the United States, Hillary and Tenzing, upon reaching the peak, would have been greeted by a large sign reading: KEEP OFF —THIS MEANS YOU!

After following the fence a certain number of miles, you come to an opening protected by a cattle guard—a western invention consisting of a number of rails laid across the road over a shallow trench. Vehicles can negotiate this kind of open-work bridge, but stock won't try it for fear of getting their hoofs caught between the rails; so it serves the purpose of a gate without having to be opened and closed for each passing car. While bouncing over this guard, you'll see another sign: PRIVATE ROAD—KEEP OUT! *Johnson Land and Cattle Co.* The name isn't Johnson, of course, but never mind. The road is gravel and fairly rough. It leads back among the dry and barren foothills, out of sight of the main highway, and runs, finally, past a large, paved parking lot and up to a gate in another fence, this one of steel mesh twelve feet high topped by three strands of barbed wire on a slanting bracket. At this point a Marine guard with a gun steps out of a little house and asks where the hell you think you're going.

Beyond him you see a number of low government buildings—government architecture has an unmistakable look— and that's all you'll see, and all I am permitted to tell you. If you want to know more, ask any waitress in any restaurant in Albuquerque. She'll have more dope on it than I do, anyway; I have to go through channels to get my information.

The conference took a couple of hours, and was as productive as most emergency conferences that are called on the spur of the moment by an administrative officer in a big tizzy, before enough data has been assembled to act upon. We finally came to the momentous decision that we had better wait until Jack Bates, who had been flown to Nevada by the Army, got back with some accurate information, and adjourned. I drove home, parked the Pontiac in the driveway, and let myself into the house. The lights were on in the living room, and Natalie was sprawled in the big chair with her glasses on and not much else: she was wearing one of those abbreviated nighties that come equipped with little pants, and need them. She looked about ten years old.

I said, "That's a hell of a costume for a married woman. You look like Shirley Temple."

She sat up quickly, startled. Absorbed in her book, she had not heard me come in. Then she grinned. "That shows *your* age," she said. "I'm younger than she is."

"What are you reading?" I asked.

She glanced at the cover of the book and shrugged. "Just brushing up on how to save the world," she said. "All it needs is one or two little changes in human nature, it says here."

She took off her glasses and laid them aside, shivered slightly and reached for the short white terry-cloth robe she had thrown off. "It was hot in here while the fire was going," she said. "I didn't realize it had burned down so far. How did your meeting go?"

I shrugged. "We accomplished the usual amount of nothing."

"Trouble, darling?"

"Uh-huh."

"Who was there, or shouldn't I ask?"

"Shouldn't ask," I said. "The Director was there; I'll tell you that much. He was very happy. He loves trouble, as long as it happens to somebody else."

"To you?"

"Oh, no," I said. "He wouldn't like that. It might reflect back on him. No, I'm in the clear. In fact, I'm apt to come out of this very well." I hesitated; but there are times when you have to talk to someone. "You see, Princess, somebody in Washington didn't like a few recommendations I made in my last report. Apparently that's what's been holding things up for the past six months. When they hear things they don't like in Washington, they have a routine they go into. First they decide that the guy who gave the unpalatable advice must be a subversive bastard, or he wouldn't say unpleasant things like that. And then they look around for somebody who'll give them the answer they want. Well, it's never hard to find a man who'll tell a Senator what he wants to hear. Only now it turns out that I was right after all."

She looked relieved. "Then you should feel very good about it, darling."

I nodded. "Sure," I said. "I feel swell about it. I just

love to have a hundred and sixty-three men die to prove me right. Good night, Princess."

"Greg!"

I looked back. "They tested it, Princess," I said softly. "I told them we didn't know enough yet, but they tested it anyway. It wiped out Northrop and his whole crew. That's very confidential information, so don't tell anybody I told you. Just how they're going to keep a hundred and sixty-three families from learning papa's dead. . . .!" I drew a long breath. "Good night, Princess. I've got a date with a nightmare."

I went down the hall to my room. Early in our marriage we had discovered that, both being temperamental and used to privacy, we got more sleep and family harmony by occupying separate rooms except on special occasions. Natalie, therefore, had the big master bedroom adjoining the bathroom; while I used the smaller of the two rooms across the hall for sleeping, and the larger as a combination gunroom, trophy room, and study—it also was supplied with a studio couch so that it could serve as guest room when needed. My bedroom was fairly bare; I had resisted all Natalie's efforts to have it decorated. I don't like to feel that I'm part of an artistic composition when I'm trying to sleep. I got out of my clothes and into pajamas, went into the bathroom and took a one-and-a-half-grain Nembutal —all the propaganda against barbiturates notwithstanding, there's nothing like a sedative when you really need to sleep—and went to bed. I lay there for about an hour before the pill went to work.

Then there was this red light flashing in the middle of the instrument board and with each flash the warning bells would scream throughout the building and everybody else was running away but I couldn't move a muscle. I woke up sweating. The light was on and Natalie was bending over me.

"It's Larry on the phone again," she said.

I said, "If the wires blew down, he'd die of frustration. What does he want now? Incidentally, what's the time?"

"Twelve-thirty. He wants you to come over."

"Over where?"

"His house. Jack's there. Larry says he's in bad shape. Drunk or something. Larry wants you to talk to him."

I said, "Do you mind driving me? I'm full of Nembutal."

"Don't be silly," she said. "I'll be ready as soon as you are."

SEVEN

IT WAS ONE of those brilliantly clear nights they often have out here, particularly in winter. You could see more stars than an easterner ever dreamed of. It was cold, and I was glad Natalie had handed me my big, fur-collared, down-insulated hunting jacket instead of some more refined garment. Herself she had wrapped in the usual minks. The heater of the Pontiac had barely time to start functioning properly before we reached our destination.

"Should I wait out here?" Natalie asked.

I looked at the lighted windows. "It looks as if everybody's up. You can come on in and talk to Ruth."

She grimaced. "That'll be a real treat," she said and got out of the car. I closed the door after her. As we moved up the walk, she took my arm, saying, "I'm sorry. I'll be good. I've been very good lately, haven't I?"

"Is that what it is?" I asked. "I noticed you hadn't been acting at all natural."

She laughed, squeezing my arm. "Darling, that's what I love about you. You're such a *rewarding* person to do things for."

The house looked about like ours, except that it was peach-colored and somewhat smaller. It gave out a sound of organ music, which seemed a little odd under the circumstances; but Larry was a hi-fi bug and needed very little excuse to turn on the system. I saw the chunky shape of Jack Bates's station wagon in the driveway; it was a red Willys with high-altitude head, oversized radiator and clutch, and four-wheel drive. I knew all about it because I had been invited to come along some Sunday and make my fortune—prospecting was his most recent enthusiasm—but I get enough of uranium and its by-products at work without spending my spare time looking for more.

Ruth met us at the door. She was wearing what seemed to be one of Larry's old shirts and a pair of faded blue jeans—the western substitute for slacks, shorts, housedresses,

riding pants, and just about any other practical garment
you can think of. They'd use them for bathing suits if they
had any water to swim in. Ruth's were rolled to just below
the knees, and had a good deal of paint on them, as did
the shirt.

"You're going to have to forgive the way I look," she
said. "Everything's been so . . . so hectic tonight I knew
I couldn't sleep so I've been in the studio working like
mad."

We were shedding our coats. I asked, "Where are they?"

She gestured toward the sound of music. "They're waiting for you in the living room, Greg. I'll take Natalie into
my private sanctum if she doesn't mind an awful mess. I
never do seem to get things organized . . . Oh, dear, don't
treat that lovely coat like that; let me hang it up in the
closet!"

I left them being sweet to each other. When I opened
the living-room door, the organ music almost knocked me
down. I could feel the bass vibrations through the soles of
my feet. The DeVry living room had an unbalanced look;
no arrangement of furniture could shift the center of gravity
far from the big, homemade corner enclosure that housed
Larry's loud-speaker system. At the other end of the room
from the monstrosity, Larry and Jack were sitting side by
side on the maple sofa without speaking. They had empty
glasses on the low maple table in front of them—neatly
set on coasters. As far as I'm concerned, there are two
kinds of hospitality. One lets you set your drink down where
you damn well please, trusting you to use a little judgment; the other keeps running after you with coasters.
Strangely, this never used to bother me back in Chicago;
but like many things about the DeVrys, it had started to
get on my nerves lately.

I had the illusion that Larry and Jack looked small and
far away, dwarfed by the giant sounds emanating from
the contraption in the corner. The reproduction was really
very good, as a matter of fact; if you closed your eyes
you could almost imagine that you had the organ in your
lap. Larry must have felt the jar as I closed the door. He
certainly couldn't have heard the sound, but he looked up,
jumped up, and came over.

"Greg!" he shouted, shaking my hand as if he hadn't
seen me for months. "Glad you're here! Come over and
talk some sense into this guy." I think that's what he said;

it was hard to make out over the noise. I made some gesture toward the roaring and screaming speakers. Larry walked over and cut the thing off. The silence was tremendous. "Just showing Jack the effect of my new dividing network," he said. "Sit down, Greg. I'll get some more beer."

"None for me," I said. "Coffee if you've got it."

He nodded, and left the room. I walked across the rug in the unearthly silence and sat down in a chair not far from Jack. He was making a thing of lighting a cigarette. I leaned back and waited. There were some of Ruth's paintings on the walls. Back east she had done all right with her landscapes, but out here she couldn't seem to get the size of the country. The dunes at White Sands looked like Jackson Park Beach in Chicago. She did better with flowers. There was a cholla cactus in bloom—the red, not the yellow —that I hadn't seen before. I reminded myself to say something nice about it as an exercise in diplomacy, before we left.

"I'm quitting, Greg," Jack said.

I looked at him for a moment. I had noticed that he had been looking kind of worn and preoccupied Christmas Eve; he looked worse now. He was wearing boots, jeans, and a red wool shirt—they run those tests off in pretty rough country. There was nothing to be gained by taking it big. I said, "This is a hell of a time of night for it."

"I wrote up my report on the plane coming back," he said. "I stopped by at the Project on the way. Van Horn was there; I turned it over to him. You can read it in the morning. I've had it, Greg."

"Okay," I said. " 'By, kid."

"I mean it," he said. "I'm not kidding."

"I'm not arguing with you," I said.

"Is that the way you feel about it?"

"Do my feelings enter into the equation?"

"Well," he said, "a little. You brought me out here. I appreciate that. It was a big opportunity, and I've tried to do my best by it. Also, you're a . . . oh, hell, you're a pretty good guy, and we've had a lot of fun together. I hate to run off and leave you in a spot just when everybody's going to be wanting results. But I've got to do it, Greg." He got up and walked to the picture window and parted the drapes and looked out at nothing in particular. "I've just come from there," he said quietly. "You don't know what it's like. It's . . . it's a hundred square miles of . . . of nothing. Nothing but glass."

"Glass?"

"Volcanic glass. Stuff like obsidian. What you get when molten rock cools too quickly to crystallize." He had been reading up on geology since he caught the uranium fever.

"A hundred miles of glass," I said.

"That's right."

"How thick?"

"Several feet, at least."

"But not more than several feet?"

He glanced at me. "No. It followed the surface, all right, just as you figured it would."

"Hot?"

"Temperature or radioactivity?"

"Both."

"We couldn't get on it. It was still smoking. Radioactivity wasn't enough to worry about, except for the usual high readings near ground zero, from the trigger explosion. They sent a 'copter in to check; also to look for any signs of Northrop and his team. They didn't find anything. No block house, no observation posts, nothing. Just glass." He drew a long breath. "Looks like you had it figured about right. It ought to make quite a weapon—if you can learn how to control it."

"But you aren't going to help?"

He shook his head. "I've had it, Greg. I don't want any part of it from now on. To be honest with you, I'm scared stiff."

I looked at him, and shifted my gaze to Ruth's cactus. She had not got the red quite right after all. The real flower had a tinge of purple.

"Jack," I said, "what stopped it?"

He shook his head again. "I don't know. What stops a chain reaction in an unlimited mass of material? God, maybe."

"That doesn't help much," I said. "We can't draft Him. Besides, Washington would probably turn Him down as a security risk. After all, isn't He related to that well-known radical Jesus Christ?"

Jack said, "It doesn't mean anything to you, does it? A hundred square miles of the face of the earth fused to nothing. . . . What if it *hadn't* stopped, Greg? Have you thought of that?"

I said, "It had occurred to me."

"One of the aerial observers said it looked as if some-body had dropped a coal on a piece of brown paper. You know how paper will sometimes char and glow for a while, a kind of hole growing away from the central point. And sometimes it will go out of its own accord. And some-times . . . sometimes, if a breath of air strikes it just right, maybe, it will burst into flames—"

"Jack," I said, "you're playing games with words. You're trying to equate a simple reaction involving cellulose and oxygen with a very complex reaction involving—"

"Involving the earth itself." He swung around to face me. "You don't know why it stopped this time, do you? Or what it's going to do next time?"

I said, "All I know is that we need to know more about it."

"All I know," he said, "is that we know too much about it already. So I'm quitting. Mrs. Bates didn't bring up her boy to set the world on fire. . . . Greg, fly out there. Go take a look at it. It's hard and kind of slick and brown, except for places that have bubbles like that Mexican glass. Nothing else as far as you can see: no trees, no grass, not even any rocks. Just this hard, shiny, smoking stuff, clear to the horizon. You can stand there and think about what might have happened if it hadn't stopped. Just a dead glass ball, spinning through space like a damn Christmas orna-ment."

I said, "Jack, if a thing is in the realm of possible hu-man knowledge, it's going to get itself discovered sooner or later, whether the human race is ready for it or not."

He said, "I've heard that argument. And the one about do we want the Russians to get it first. I don't want any-body to get it. But one guy is not going to get it for sure, and that's me. I can't stop your going ahead with it, or the Russians going ahead with it, or anybody else who likes to tinker with the celestial works. But *I* don't have to be the one to discover it. I don't have to have it on *my* conscience."

I said, "Well, good luck, kid. I hope you and your con-science have lots and lots of fun."

I got up and walked across the room and into the hall without looking back. I retrieved my jacket and my wife and got out of there. The cold night air hit me outside the door. I stopped to zip the jacket up, and regarded the jeep station wagon in the drive with an envious eye. That's my idea of what a vehicle should look like, instead of a chrome-plated thunderbolt on wheels. He even had a winch on the front so that if he got stuck he could run the cable to a tree and haul himself out. The only trouble with that idea is the scarcity of trees in most parts of the country where they hunt uranium.

Natalie said, "Can you tell me what it's all about?"

"Jack's quitting," I said.

"Why?"

"He's scared, I guess," I said. "He's got an attack of conscience, like old man Fischer. He wants us to leave it to God."

She hesitated; then she said, "Darling, he could be right."

I grinned and took her arm. "You're a big help," I said. "Besides, what makes you think God wants to be bothered? After all, it's not much of a planet. He's got lots bigger ones."

EIGHT

I AWOKE WITH a slight headache in a bed that seemed momentarily unfamiliar to me; and the ceiling above me was white stucco instead of the blue I was accustomed to seeing in the mornings. I don't care for stucco walls and ceilings, but when you've got them there isn't a hell of a lot you can do about them. While I was orienting myself and recalling the events of the night, the door opened and Natalie came in, bearing a tray.

"Are you awake, darling?" she asked.

"Uh-huh," I said, sitting up in the big double bed that had no head or foot. "What time is it, anyway?"

"Almost eleven. Thursday."

She set the tray on the dresser and came over. She was fully dressed in her favorite around-the-house costume, which consisted of gray flannel Bermuda shorts, a man's striped shirt, knee-length wool socks, and nicely polished loafers. The logic of baring your legs with shorts only to cover them again with long socks escapes me. Her dark hair was smooth and shining, and her face had a scrubbed and glowing look. If I had remembered nothing at all about what had happened after we got home, I would have known by looking at her: sex always seemed to agree with her.

She bent down to kiss me lightly, and grinned. "Well," she said, "we had a hard time getting you to sleep last night, but you certainly made up for it this morning. How do you feel?"

"Who had a hard time doing what?" I asked. She looked pretty but somewhat too fashionable and proper. I reached out and grabbed the leg of her shorts, threw her off balance, set her down hard on the bed, and caught her as she bounced. I kissed her vigorously to the detriment of her neatly applied lipstick. "I feel fine," I said.

"Relax, Buster," she said, pushing at me. "Your breakfast is getting cold." Her voice sounded a little odd, and her efforts to escape did not carry conviction. We wrestled

49

briefly, I kissed her again, and from there we proceeded to more adult occupations. "I should have known better than to marry a genius," she breathed at last. "Six months of the year he doesn't know I exist, and the rest of the time it isn't safe to go near him." She rubbed her chin. "Darling, if I might make a suggestion, it would be nice if you shaved before you let passion get the better of you."

I grinned. She sat up and pulled up her socks, put her feet back into her loafers, and got up to retrieve the other discarded portions of her attire. She went to the dresser for a fresh shirt to replace the one that had got rumpled, and disappeared into the bathroom. I got up and brought the tray back to the bed and began to eat. Presently she returned, looking serene and untouched and radiant. She poured herself some coffee and sat on the edge of the bed to drink it.

"I think I'm going to do this room over," she said abruptly.

I looked around judiciously. It was a black-and-white room, very, very severe and modern and not my idea of a lady's boudoir, but what the hell? When I was in here my mind was generally not on interior decoration; the rest of the time I had my own room.

"Go ahead," I said.

"I think. . . . Darling, how's your stomach?"

I glanced at her. "My stomach's swell. Why do you ask?"

"I shouldn't have let you have those drinks last night. Are you sure you're feeling all right?"

I said, "I'm fine, Princess. You've been asking me if I'm all right for the past five months."

"I know," she said. "I guess. I just feel . . . kind of responsible for you. Greg?"

"Yes?"

"Please be careful."

"What are you driving at?"

She said, "I'm driving at that I love you and don't want anything to happen to you. That's what I'm driving at."

We were not in the habit of throwing the word "love" around very much, perhaps because it gets such a thorough workout from other people.

I cleared my throat and said, "I'm healthy as a pup, Natalie. Stop worrying about me. I've got it made. Honest."

She shook her head quickly. "That isn't what I mean—"

The sound of the doorbell interrupted her. We've got a

refined one that plays four musical notes, but it still won't open the door and tell the man we don't want any. Natalie drained her cup and set it on the tray.

"I'll see who it is. Finish your breakfast."

The chimes played their little ding-dong tune again as she went out of the room. I heard her cross the living room, open the door, and speak to someone outside. Whoever it was came in, the front door closed, and I heard her say, "Just sit down somewhere. I'll tell him."

Then she came down the hall and into the room. "It's Van Horn, darling. He wants to see you."

"What about?"

"He didn't say. Better wash your face. You're still kind of lipsticky."

She tossed my dressing gown at me, as I got out of the bed and found my slippers. When I came into the living room, Van Horn was sitting on one of our less comfortable chairs, looking a little like a man waiting to sell the lady of the house a new vacuum cleaner. There was a long, paper-wrapped package across his knees.

I said, "Hi, Van. What can I do for you? What have you got there?"

He said, "I want you to identify something for me, if possible."

"Sure," I said. I cleared a couple of ash trays and a bowl of flowers from the cocktail table. "You can make your demonstration here, Professor."

He said reprovingly, "This is a fairly serious matter, Dr. Gregory." In all the time I had known him, I had never heard him address any of us by our first names, although we all called him Van. I guess it's easier to be a cop if you don't allow yourself to be too friendly with the suspects. And don't ever kid yourself; to a security agent, everybody is a suspect, all the time.

I said, "You're the one who's making a big mystery of it, not I. How about a cup of coffee?"

"No, thanks." He rose and laid his package on the long, low table, produced a small penknife, and cut the tape that held the brown paper in place. He looked up. "I would like you to take your time and be sure before you say anything."

I nodded. Natalie, who was standing beside me, put her hand on my arm. She looked a little scared. I could hardly blame her. After the build-up, I probably looked a little scared myself. Van Horn pulled the paper apart. It was a twelve-gauge Remington automatic shotgun with a compensator on the muzzle. The short spreader tube was in place. I'm not very fond of automatics, and I can live indefinitely without compensators, poly-chokes, or muzzlebrakes in any shape or form, but some people like them and do very well with them. It was not the gun itself that made Natalie gasp, however, but the stuff that was on it. Well, I had seen blood before; even blood with dirt and pine needles drying in it.

"Turn it over," I said.

Van Horn put a finger under the trigger guard, and exposed the other side of the weapon.

I said, "It's Jack Bates's gun. You don't have to take my word for it. All his hunting equipment is insured. The serial number will be on the policy and in the company's files, so I'm not giving away any secrets."

"Good enough," said Van Horn. "Is there anything else you'd care to say about it?"

I leaned over and sniffed the slotted barrel of the compensator, where fouling is most apt to collect. The gun had been fired recently enough for the odor of burned powder to remain sharp and noticeable. I shook my head.

"Not without knowing more about the situation," I said. "Except—"

"Except what, Dr. Gregory?"

I walked over to the telephone table in the hall, found a roll of scotch tape in the drawer, returned, and dropped it in front of him.

"Except that I don't like your approach," I said. "Cover it up again, Van, and stop playing cop around here. Jack Bates is a friend of mine. Don't come around here and shove his bloody gun under my nose without telling me what's happened to him! I ought to wrap the damn thing around your neck!"

He asked quietly, "What makes you think something has happened to Dr. Bates?"

I said, "What am I supposed to think? That he chopped the head off a chicken, let it bleed all over his gun, and then presented the piece to you as a souvenir?"

"You have no other reason for worrying about him?"

"Such as?"

"His disturbed condition last night, for instance." Van Horn paused, and grimaced. "I guess I am beating around the bush. After leaving the DeVrys' house last night, Dr. Bates apparently went home, packed his station wagon with camping equipment, and drove to a public camp ground up in the Sandias, on the road to the ski-run. He had the place to himself at this time of year. This morning, however, some kids driving up to go skiing pulled into the area to put chains on—the road's pretty slick up above. This was about eight-thirty. They saw Dr. Bates's car, and while the boys were working, the girls kind of strolled over to look around. They found him lying behind the car, dead. He had been shot in the face. The gun was beside him."

"I see," I said. I looked down at the shotgun on the table and felt a little funny. After all, I had sat in quite a few blinds and pits along the river with that automatic and the man who had owned it, in the past three years. I had sworn at the muzzle-blast of that damn compensator, and griped about the gun's habit of tossing its fired shells into the face of whoever was standing to the right of it. I had also watched it knock three mallards out of a decoying formation—like busting pipes in a shooting gallery— and reach into the sky an incredible distance and fold up a Canada goose flying far overhead. With a rifle, I could usually hold my own against Jack Bates, and maybe do a little better at long range, since he was fundamentally a snapshooter rather than a marksman; but when it came to shotgunning, he was an artist, and I didn't even try to compete. Well, that was a good enough epitaph for a hunting man, I reflected. I said, "It's funny nobody heard the shot. That's a game refuge up there and they're kind of sensitive about having guns go off."

Van Horn said, "As a matter of fact, a forest service truck came along a little later. One of the men living a few miles below had heard the report while he was shaving, but he'd gone looking up the wrong canyon first. He puts the time as just about daybreak. Unfortunately, by the time he arrived and took charge, the kids had already flagged down a couple of other cars and people had walked all over the place."

I frowned at the gun. "Was it buckshot?" I asked.

He hesitated. Policemen are all alike, even when you put them into gabardine suits and fancy government jobs. They never like to answer questions for fear they might accidentally give somebody a break.

"Yes," he said. "Why?"

"Jack had a habit of loading up his shotgun at night—Number One buck, usually—and keeping it handy when he was camping out. We had arguments about it. I never like a loaded gun in camp."

"I see. Was this habit of his well known?"

I shrugged. "I may have kidded him about it with other people listening. Anybody who'd camped with him overnight would know it, of course."

Van Horn nodded. "You talked to him last night, I understand. He was resigning his position at the Project, is that right? According to Dr. DeVry, he was upset about"—he glanced at Natalie, who was not cleared for confidential information—"about what he'd seen in Nevada. I noticed something of the sort myself; but I only saw him for a moment when he stopped by my office to leave his report. I'd like your opinion: would you say he was disturbed enough to kill himself?"

I said, "That's a stupid damn question, Van. If I'd thought so last night, I'd have done something about it, wouldn't I?"

"Not if you were too annoyed with him for quitting to consider the possibility."

"Thanks," I said, "for reminding me. Actually, he seemed pretty well under control to me. He'd made his decision to quit, and that took care of the situation."

Van Horn touched the gun lightly. "The safety is off," he said, "which indicates it was fired deliberately, not by accident. Everything adds up to suicide, Dr. Gregory, except for one thing. The police surgeon says that, judging by the distribution of the pellets and the lack of powder burns, Dr. Bates was shot from a distance of at least eight feet."

There was a little sound from Natalie. I may have made some similar noise myself. Van Horn went on in his deliberate and pedantic way: "Even if he had arranged an elaborate method of killing himself by remote control—and suicides will rig up some fancy devices; God only knows what goes on in their minds during the final few minutes—we can't quite see how the gun, which would naturally recoil even further away from him, got back to be found beside his body. Furthermore, there are no fingerprints on the weapon at all, not even Dr. Bates's. Somebody wiped it quite clean." He cleared his throat. "Under the circumstances, the police feel that a thorough investigation is indicated. I've persuaded them to let me handle it as far as Project personnel is concerned, since I know the people involved, and since there are some security angles that have to be treated with discretion." He looked up. "You understand, this is a favor the authorities are doing us. If I can't satisfy them, they'll put their own men on the job."

I glanced at Natalie, still standing beside me, and patted her hand. "Well, we haven't killed anybody, have we, Princess?" I said, and looked back to Van Horn. "Ask your questions."

"Your talk with Dr. Bates last night," he said, "wasn't exactly friendly, was it?"

I said, "We didn't fight, but I'm afraid I wasn't as sympathetic as I might have been. I get fed up with that point of view."

"What point of view is that?"

"Putting one man's tender conscience ahead of . . . Oh, hell, let's not get into philosophy, Van. Maybe that's the only way to deal with these problems; just hide your head in the sand and pretend they don't exist. Or wash your hands of them and let other people take the blame for discovering what's inevitably going to be discovered anyway. Are you suggesting that I drove up into the mountains this morning and shot Jack because he wouldn't work for us any longer? That would seem rather illogical, wouldn't it? Alive, he might have changed his mind; dead, he certainly won't be any help."

He said, "You're referring rather callously to a man you claim to have been your friend, Dr. Gregory."

I said, "I'll do my weeping in private. You let me worry about that. What else do you want to know? We left the DeVrys' about one-thirty, drove straight home, and haven't been out of the house since. That's called an alibi, I think."

"Yes," he said. "Can you prove it?"

I said, "Only if you take Natalie's word for it; and I suppose she would lie for me if I asked her to."

He said, "It's not a question of Mrs. Gregory's veracity, but of her knowledge. My understanding is that you don't share the same bedroom."

I looked at him sharply. "You seem to know a lot about our private life."

"That's my business, Dr. Gregory."

"Yes," I said, "I suppose it is. However, your information is slightly at fault, Van. We do share the same room occasionally, and last night was one of the occasions."

He said to Natalie, "Is that right, Mrs. Gregory?"

She said, "Yes. Greg was home from one-thirty on; I can swear to that. He'd taken a sleeping pill about an hour and a half before Larry DeVry called him. Being waked up, and having to dress and go out, and getting upset about Jack's quitting all combined to give him a fine case of the jitters. We finally had a couple of drinks together—this must have been around three o'clock—and went to bed in my room, with lewd intentions which you'll be pleased to know were satisfactorily carried out. I woke up early, but Greg was still sleeping soundly half an hour ago. I can vouch for the fact that he wasn't shooting anybody up in the mountains at dawn."

Van Horn nodded. "Yes," he said. "But from your account it's obvious that being sound asleep all morning, he can't do the same for you, Mrs. Gregory."

Natalie looked startled. "Oh," she said, "do I need an alibi?"

"The police seem to think so," Van Horn said. "It seems that they found this hanging in a tree near Dr. Bates's body." He reached into his pocket and brought out the bright silk scarf Natalie had worn out driving the day before.

No one said anything as he came forward and spread the scarf on the low table beside the gun, pushing the brown paper aside to give himself more space. The paper crackled loudly in the silent room. The scarf, although of more expensive material, closely resembled one of those multi-colored squares of thin silk all the teen-agers were wearing on their heads or around their necks; there was no reason why I should have recognized it with such certainty, but I did. I could remember the way she had pulled it off her hair as she walked across the living room yesterday to answer the phone that was Larry asking me to come to the Project immediately. Since I had last seen the scarf, somebody had punched a ragged, ugly hole near one corner of it.

Natalie took a step forward and touched the silk with the tip of her finger. "Hanging in a tree?" she asked softly. "May I ask how?"

"It was stuck on a dead stub about six feet off the ground. You can see the hole."

She looked up. Her eyes were candid and innocent. "I

don't understand," she said. "How does this scarf concern me, Mr. Van Horn?"

He said, "I was under the impression it was yours, Mrs. Gregory."

"I don't know why you should be," she said calmly. "I've never seen it before in my life."

NINE

I SAW HIM out with his package, and closed the door gently behind him—doing, I thought, a pretty good job with my face and voice. When I came back into the living room, Natalie was still standing there, awaiting me.

She said, "Do me a favor, darling. Say anything you like, but don't be corny. *Please* don't be corny."

I said, "He didn't believe you."

"Naturally not," she said. "He's probably got six secret agents who'll swear in court that they've seen me wear the lousy thing. But it stopped him, didn't it? Without coming right out and calling me a liar, he couldn't go ahead and ask the other questions on his mind. And I just didn't feel like answering his damn questions, darling." She looked up at me defiantly. "Or yours either."

"I haven't asked any," I said.

She said, "The fact is, I don't know how that damn scarf got there. And I don't want to guess. And I'm not going to help him guess. Or you. Or the police. Or anybody. What are they trying to prove, anyway? I'm five feet four and a half inches tall. Am I supposed to have got up on a stepladder so that I could lose my scarf six feet off the ground? Or do they think I slipped out of the house this morning, drove up into the mountains and committed murder, hung my scarf up in a tree so everybody'd know who'd done it, and came rushing back to give my husband breakfast in bed? Is that what *you* think, darling?"

I said, "It's not my problem."

"What do you mean?"

"I mean," I said, "I'm not a policeman. I don't give a damn if your name is Booth and you murdered Lincoln. I don't have to worry about it. I'm the one person in the world who doesn't have to worry about it. As your husband, I don't think I could be made to testify even if I'd seen you come in dripping blood; certainly I'm not obliged to play amateur detective in my own house. So just relax, Princess, and stop snapping at me like a Pekinese. Naturally, I wouldn't mind being taken into your confidence —assuming that you actually have something to confide and aren't just acting mysterious for fun—but all I really want to know is whether or not you know what the hell you're doing. After all, the man wasn't accusing you of murder. All he wanted was a reasonable explanation of a rather curious phenomenon. By lying about it, you make it look very big and important. Is that what you want?"

She said, "I don't care how it looks, darling. And I know precisely what I'm doing."

"Swell," I said. "In that case, let's just close the discussion and have a cup of coffee."

"It's cold by now," she said. "I'll take it out into the kitchen and warm it up. . . . Greg?"

"Yes?"

"What would you do if you learned I had killed him?"

I said, "I'd keep my trap shut. Did you?"

"What do you think?"

I looked at her for a moment. She was far away from me. She might have killed somebody, at that. I suppose everybody is capable of it. I had killed a man once myself.

I said, "If you want to tell me, either way, go ahead and tell me. But I'm not going to play games with it."

"You're not *sure*, are you, darling?"

I said, "I'm sure of this: if you look me in the eye and tell me you didn't, I'll take your word for it. As long as you keep talking around it, I'll reserve my opinion."

She said, "What motive would I have for killing Jack Bates?"

"You go to hell, sweetheart," I said. "I could make up a list of motives as long as your arm, both clean and dirty, for any woman around here to kill any man around here. Do you want me to lie and say they don't apply to you?"

She laughed. "All right, darling. You shave and get dressed. I'll warm up the coffee; or would you rather have lunch? It's past noon."

"I just finished breakfast," I said. "Although it seems quite a while ago."

"Greg."

"Yes?"

She looked up at me. "I'm sorry," she said. "Honest. I didn't mean for anything like this to happen, and I'd tell you about it if I could, but . . ." She shook her head quickly. "I know it looks screwy, but I do know what I'm doing. Now."

I said, "The apology is accepted. The explanation is rejected as confused and inadequate. Don't make little cryptic speeches at me, Princess. Either say something or shut up."

"I am saying something," she said. "I'm saying good-by."

Everyone has his own way of taking these things; mine, perfected over a period of thirty-four years, might be called the poker-face technique. After all, a man looks pretty silly with his mouth hanging open. There are times when it might be more diplomatic to show a little reaction; if you don't jump to their bombshells, people are apt to think you don't care. However, I learned as a kid in the woods, hunting with older men, to keep from yelping when I stubbed my toe or cracked my head; and it's one of the lessons you don't unlearn very easily.

I let enough time go by to make sure my voice would work properly, and said, "Come back again when you can stay a little longer."

She said, "Sometimes I wonder how tough you really are, darling. You have a very nice protective coating, I will say that for you. Well, it's nice to hit a man who can take it."

"Uh-huh," I said. "I'm glad you enjoy it. Where are you going?"

"Reno. I should never have come back."

"I can see that. Now." I studied her for a moment. "This sudden departure is apt to look very funny to a lot of men with badges who don't understand your impulsive nature."

She said, "Darling, will you stop telling me how things are going to look! And why be bitter? You wouldn't have had half as much fun playing invalid without me." She drew a long, uneven breath. "We probably should never have got married in the first place. You're really a very dull and demanding man to live with, most of the time. And this God-forsaken country, and the ghastly people . . .! Besides, theoretically I disapprove of you, and that's not right. A woman should be proud of her husband's work, shouldn't she?"

"Aren't you?"

She shook her head. "You're a very fine scientist, I have no doubt, but"—she hesitated—"but you have no sense of moral responsibility whatsoever. What you're doing is wrong, darling, wrong, wrong, wrong! You're doing a terrible thing; why can't you see it?"

I said, "You're referring to the Project—"

"You know what I'm referring to."

I said slowly, "Princess, I've never denied the possibility that I might be wrong. One of the revealing things about this Davy Crockett character is that saying of his: 'Be sure you're right—then go ahead.' It takes a man of very limited imagination to be sure he's right. I'm not at all sure. I never have been, and I probably never will be—of anything I can't prove mathematically and check in the laboratory for good measure. But it seems that every other person on this planet, including my wife, has been blessed with divine guidance on a number of subjects, including my work. It's a pity the good Lord hasn't seen fit to take me into His confidence as well!" I caught my breath; it was one of those times when even breathing seemed to require conscious effort. "Do you want me to quit, Natalie? Is that what you want?"

She shook her head quickly. "No. I couldn't ask you; and if I did, and you agreed, we wouldn't stay married very long, anyway, would we? You wouldn't respect me for blackmailing you; and I wouldn't respect you for letting yourself be blackmailed."

I said, "But your ideal is a man who buries his head in the sand like an ostrich—or even commits suicide—rather than face some cold hard physical facts that the human race is inevitably going to have to face, sooner or later?"

"It hasn't been proved that Jack killed himself," she said.

I glanced at her, surprised. "I wasn't thinking of Jack. I was thinking of old man Fischer. Why, have you discussed this with Jack? You're talking pretty much like he was last night when he told me he was quitting."

She hesitated, and her eyes were not quite candid when she replied, "We may have talked about it some time. It's a fairly common subject of conversation around here."

I said, "Not common enough, apparently. You may have talked a lot about it to Jack Bates, although I wasn't aware that the two of you went in for philosophical discussions. But in three years of marriage, this is the first time I've been told that you actually disapprove of the way I make my living. When did this moral revulsion come over you?"

"I . . . I don't know," she said. "It's just . . . kind of grown. Knowing what you were doing over there, every day. . . . I didn't say anything because I didn't want to hurt you."

I said, "Well, just brace yourself and hurt me now. Let's hear this soft-boiled reasoning that makes scientific progress a crime against humanity."

She shook her head quickly. "It's no use, darling. You know exactly what I'm going to say because you've heard it from a lot of other people. And I know exactly what you're going to say because I've heard it from you. You're going to say that you might as well go on working on this terrible project of yours because somebody will. You're going to say that what's done with the results of your work is none of your business. You're going to say that you're a physicist, not a politician or a social scientist; and that it's not your fault if other people haven't done as well in their fields as you have in yours. And you'll go right on tossing off horrible discoveries—you and people like you—with no more compunction than little boys playing with firecrackers, until you manage to destroy the whole world and everyone on it."

I started to speak, and shut up. It was obviously no use. It was like being alone in a foreign country where nobody understood your language.

I said at last, "Well, I don't see quite how we got onto this. We started out with a scarf hanging on a tree up in the Sandias. But I guess we've pretty well covered the ground, haven't we, Princess?" She didn't speak. I said, "I'll get your suitcases out of the garage. Don't forget to put gas in that toy of yours before you get out of town. It's a long haul to the next pump."

TEN

THE REST OF the day was a total loss. I was called over
to the Project around three o'clock, presumably to help
draw up a plan of action, but everybody was too busy talking about Jack Bates to get any work done. The Director
had ordered a complete inventory of all classified documents
on the Project, to see if anything was missing. Maybe he
had to do it, but it wasn't exactly a gesture of confidence;
and the whole place was buzzing with theories. The human
race contains a surprising percentage of ghouls, as you will
see demonstrated on the highway any time there's a serious
accident—they'll block traffic for an hour, even after the
ambulance is gone, just to get a look at the blood. They
were having a field day with the gory details of Jack's death.
I left as soon as I could, drove around for a while, had
dinner at a hamburger joint, and went home to bed.

I don't know what time it was when the telephone woke
me; I never did get around to looking at my watch. I
stumbled out into the hall in the dark, fished around for
the instrument, found it, and got it to my ear.

"Mr. Gregory?" a female voice said. "Is this Mr. James
Gregory, Heights 3-9180? . . . All right, go ahead, sir."
I heard the singing of miles of wire leading off into the
unknown distance in an unknown direction. "Mr. Gregory?"
a man's voice said. "Mr. Gregory, this is Sheriff McKay,
of Esmeralda County, Nevada. I'm talking from Goldfield.
There's been an accident. One of those little foreign cars
went off the road a few miles south of here and burned.
The trunk must have busted open when it rolled; we picked
up a couple of suitcases with tags identifying the owner as
. . . Are you there, Mr. Gregory?"

"Yes," I said. "I'm here."

". . . as Mrs. Natalie Walsh Gregory. You were named
as next of kin."

I said, "Is my wife—"

"We don't know whether she's hurt or not." The distant

63

voice paused, then went on: "To tell you the truth, we haven't found her yet."

There was more to the conversation, but I don't remember it clearly. I do recall phoning the airport, once the line was clear; they gave me a choice of landing in Las Vegas, a hundred and eighty miles southeast of where I wanted to be, or at Reno, two hundred and sixty miles northwest. Two charter pilots were off prospecting for uranium, and the third had a broken collarbone from falling off a ladder while painting his house. I sent off a telegram to my father-in-law, dressed, went out into the garage, and started loading the Pontiac. I never drive anywhere in that country, particularly in winter, without a sleeping bag, a little food, plenty of water, and something to cook on. Civilization gets mighty thin on some of those long and desolate roads—even the paved ones—when a storm comes up or your car decides to quit on you; it's a consolation to know that you can sit it out if you have to.

I had the big door open, the engine running, and the lights on ready to move out, when a car came down the street fast and pulled up in front, blocking the driveway. Van Horn's neat and businesslike figure emerged. He came up the lane of my headlights and around the car to my window. I pushed the button and the glass came down. Sometimes I wonder if the Russians haven't got a point about us decadent democratic weaklings, after all. Motors to open and close the windows, for God's sake!

"What do you want?" I asked.

He said, "The Army's warming up a plane for us at Kirtland Field. Grab a warm coat and come on. You're in no condition to drive eight hundred miles alone, anyway."

I said, "Never mind my condition." It would have been naïve to ask how he knew where I was going: he would only tell me it was his business to know. I turned off the motor and lights, went back to the trunk and yanked it open again. With my head inside, I said, "Thanks."

"Don't thank me," he said. "The way people keep dying and disappearing around here, I want you where I can keep an eye on you."

Airplanes usually give me the creeps, but this one didn't bother me much. I had other things to think about. At one point, I recall, Van Horn nudged me and pointed down.

He wanted to call my attention to the fact that we were over the Grand Canyon. It was daylight now, and the view was, I'll admit, quite spectacular, but it was not my day for appreciating scenery.

Goldfield is situated in a kind of bowl, surrounded by the low, naked Nevada hills. The whole bowl has been torn up by mining operations. The decaying rigs and shacks of deserted mines are dotted all over the landscape. I have heard that the town was quite a metropolis once; the scene of one of the last great American gold rushes, some time around nineteen hundred. Now only the nucleus of a city remains. There are a few small filling stations and cafés— west of the Mississippi, any restaurant is a café—some short streets of modern, inhabited residences, a school or two, and several impressive public buildings massively constructed of gray stone: Goldfield is the county seat. In one of these, we found the office of the sheriff, who drove us to the scene in a brand-new Chevrolet pickup truck. In that country, the pickup is the family vehicle; but they like to keep a jeep handy for rough going.

I got out and looked around. There were people around, and jeeps; and a small plane was circling overhead. They presumably knew what they were doing. I didn't ask them what it was. I stood there for a while. It was a desolate place. The Triumph had left the road a couple of hundred yards south of where I was standing and dug two straight furrows slantingly across the wide and shallow ditch —hardly deep enough to be called that—that bordered the highway for miles through this region. The far edge of the ditch had apparently been enough to flip it into the air at the speed it was traveling; it had struck and bounced crazily across the desert for a hundred yards, disintegrating and strewing parts and contents everywhere, and mowing down a couple of yucca or Joshua trees before coming to a halt—I never know at what point in size a yucca becomes a Joshua or vice versa.

Now it was lying there with its three remaining wheels in the air, the hood and trunk lid gone, and the red paint blistered and blackened by fire. I walked over. People were doing things to the wreck, Van Horn among them. The place was lousy with the yuccas; they grew everywhere, up and down the low rounded hills, carefully spaced, each one with plenty of room around it, never two close together. Even yuccas need water, I guess, and have to fight for enough area to survive. They grew eight to twelve feet tall, with twisted arms covered by pointed spiny leaves somewhat like the leaves at the base of a pineapple. Many were brown and withered at this time of year. They cast long distorted shadows. It was a hell of a place.

I walked to the top of the nearest hill. In the distance, at least ten miles to the east, the ground sloped down to a white patch that would be a sink into which all the water in the area ran when it rained, and then evaporated during the hot dry periods between rains, leaving a salt deposit. To the west was a low range of hills, studded with yuccas. North and south ran the highway, the only sign of civilization—if you could call it that. The civilized people driving along it kept stopping and getting out to gawk at the wreck, hoping, I guess, to see some mangled bodies. They were annoyed at the sheriff's men for keeping them at a distance.

I walked back down. Van Horn said, "Oh, there you are. We'd like a full description of what she was wearing when she left home."

I said, "A blue-and-white striped shirt, gray flannel shorts, long white socks, brown loafers. A blue leather jacket. White string driving gloves with leather palms. . . . Of course she may have changed."

He shook his head. "The time it took her to get here doesn't allow for many stops; besides I had a man following her."

"What does he say?"

"He says she stepped on the gas after leaving Vegas. At a hundred and five miles per hour he remembered his wife and baby, and let Mrs. Gregory pull ahead of him. When he got here, the car was burning, but there was no sign of a human being around. It was dark, of course. He looked around as best he could; then drove on to Goldfield to get help and report to me."

The sheriff said, "Somebody could have picked her up and rushed her to a hospital, but we've checked every place within three hundred miles."

"The timing would have had to be very close," Van Horn said. "Schneider, who was following her, said he had met no cars for an hour before he found the wreck; therefore she couldn't have been taken south. If it happened that way, she must have been picked up by somebody driving north just ahead of him—and if they had an injured girl

in the car, why didn't they stop in either Goldfield or To-
nopah? And she's not out on the desert, or the planes would
have spotted her by now. Well, I'll wait for them to
finish examining the wreck, and head on back."

"Let me know when you're ready, Mr. Van Horn, and
I'll drive you," the sheriff said.

Half an hour later we were taking off again, west into
the wind and the setting sun, from the airport that consisted mainly of a faded windsock on a weatherbeaten pole.
The pilot circled and put us on course. The events of the
day had left me behind. Part of me was still sitting in a
house in Albuquerque holding a telephone. I seemed to
have caught a cold somewhere along the line, and I had
the thick, fuzzy-headed feeling that went with it.

"Do you want to hear about the wreck?" Van Horn
asked, beside me.

"What about it?" We had to shout to make ourselves
heard over the sound of the engine.

"It was a phony," he said. "There were a good many
indications of this, of course. Have you ever examined the
scene of a *real* accident, Dr. Gregory? You mentioned that
your wife was wearing loafer shoes, the kind that slip on
without lacing. She had a purse with her; you didn't mention this, but it's in Schneider's report. It's highly improb-
able that she could have been flung clear of a car traveling at that rate of speed and still retain her shoes and
purse; yet they were not found on the scene. And considering the fact that it was dark at the time, it seems unlikely that, stunned and bruised at the very least, she could
have retrieved them by herself. Of course, this hypothetical
good Samaritan might have picked them up for her, but
even that doesn't seem too plausible. But there are more
definite indications that the accident was staged, Dr. Gregory. The car had a four-speed transmission, but the lever
was in third gear—the passing or acceleration gear; not the
fourth or cruising gear. And the throttle had been jammed
wide open by an ingenious arrangement which I admit
I'm not mechanically minded enough to describe to you
since I don't fully understand it myself. Nevertheless, we can
take it as a fact. When I get the full, written report, I'll
let you look at it if you wish. I don't want you to have
any doubts in your mind about this."

"Why not?"

"Because you're a valuable man, Dr. Gregory, and we

don't want you thinking that your wife was framed or treated unjustly in any way. The facts are, first, that her scarf was found by Dr. Bates's body. Second, that upon being challenged with this, she packed her belongings into her car and drove away from home. Third, that after getting out onto the desert, away from any telephones from which Schneider might have called ahead to have her intercepted, she speeded up and left him behind. And, fourth, that at a certain point she found somebody waiting for her with another car, in which she drove off, after first wrecking her car to give the impression that she had met with an accident."

"Not much of an impression," I said. "A wreck without a driver is bound to cause comment."

"Eventually," Van Horn said. "But not immediately, before it has been determined that the driver hasn't wandered off into the desert or been picked up by a passing tourist. If Schneider had simply come upon your wife's car parked along the highway, he would have realized what must have happened; and he would have called from Goldfield and had the roads blocked ahead. There are very few roads across the desert, particularly in winter when the smaller ones are apt to be impassable. Your wife and her accomplices needed time to get clear. The wreck gave it to them."

It was like talking over the plot of a movie or television show, a pastime that always bores hell out of me. We weren't talking about a smallish girl of about twenty-three with big dark eyes and long dark hair; we were talking about a criminal and her accomplices.

I said, "Just what crimes is Natalie supposed to have committed—besides murder, of course?"

"Isn't that enough?"

"Not for you," I said. "You're a security officer, Van. You don't care if half the population of the United States is massacred in bed, as long as they don't tell any secrets while they're dying."

He said, "Fischer, you, Justin, Bates, and now Mrs. Gregory. All people connected with the Project. After a certain number of such incidents, even a security officer becomes interested, Dr. Gregory."

"I see," I said. "You smell a conspiracy?"

"Let's say that I see the outlines of a pattern."

"And the predominant color of that pattern," I said, "would it be red?"

He said, "Who else but the communists would go to such lengths to interfere with our work? I have to tell you something else, Dr. Gregory. I've been watching your wife for quite a while, waiting for her to give herself away. For a little over three years, to be exact."

I glanced at him. "Go on."

He said, "As I've told you before, I don't like coincidences. I have the theory that police work—and security is just an extension of police work into a special field, of course—I have a theory that police work is largely a matter of looking for coincidences; for the man who just happens to have a fancy alibi at the time another man is killed, for the woman who just happens to adjust her stockings so as to distract the sucker's attention while his pocket is picked. And when a brilliant young scientist who has just made a discovery that promises to give us a new weapon with all the destructive force of the older nuclear bombs but with only a fraction of the radiation effect that makes these weapons potentially almost as dangerous for the user as the target—when, at just this point in his life, such a man suddenly just 'happens' to meet an enigmatic young lady from a different walk of life entirely, who in spite of the difference in their backgrounds and interests, just happens to fall madly in love with him—"

I said, "If you don't watch it, Van, you're going to lose track of that sentence. It's a lulu already."

He said, "I know. My sentences get very involved when I'm embarrassed, Dr. Gregory. And I don't like to talk to a man about his wife."

"Then don't strain yourself," I said. "You've made your point. I'll keep it in mind. Now shut up and let me get some sleep."

ELEVEN

THE FOLLOWING DAY, I was called to the Project and informed by the Director that, much as he regretted having to take this step, he was suspending me from my duties until further notice. My mind had been too busy with other problems to consider this possibility, so it came as something of a shock; although it was, of course, a perfectly logical development. Returning home, I decided to look at the matter from its brightest side, which was that I was no longer obliged to hang around here. The car was still packed from the other night. I got an extra duffel bag of clothing, my rifle and some ammunition, all the reasonably non-perishable groceries from the kitchen, and added them to the load. Then I locked up the house and headed north.

Driving up to Santa Fe, I knew that spring was here by the fact that the whole top layer of the country was moving eastward on a gusty forty-mile breeze. That's just a zephyr in these parts; you could drop a couple of eastern hurricanes into New Mexico in the spring and nobody would notice the difference. There was dust and sand blowing hubcap-deep across the highway the whole sixty miles up U.S. 85; occasionally it would get thick enough to slow down traffic, and you could see headlights go on in the yellow murk. Then it would open up again to show you the sky clear and blue overhead, and the sun shining. The radio announced that U.S. 66 was closed for dust east of Grants. I took it easy because of the poor visibility, because I wasn't feeling too strong yet, and because those damn big wrap-around windshields cost money and you can sandblast one into frosted glass in a couple of minutes if you drive too fast through one of these disturbances.

As I approached Santa Fe, the snow-covered peaks of the Sangre de Cristos looked painfully white and clean in contrast with the dirt through which I had been driving The wind was still blowing as I drove into town, but there wasn't as much stuff flying around. I checked in at La Fonda, washed the sand off the body and brushed it out of the teeth, and went down to have dinner in the bar. It was a familiar place; Natalie and I always ate there when we were in Santa Fe. Eating alone, I got through the meal fast, went up to my room, did some research in the telephone book, went to bed, and slept all night.

In the morning I dressed myself conservatively in the light gabardine suit that's practically the uniform of the country, although you can get by on tropical worsted, or even rayon cord, if you insist. I noticed by the pants that I had lost weight, which, if I had been a little healthier, would have been cause for rejoicing: I don't like to go over two hundred. I had breakfast and spent a couple of hours driving aimlessly around town, just to see if I had company. I did. Van ought to try being followed some time, I reflected; he might understand how somebody could succumb to the temptation to stomp down on the accelerator and leave the nuisance behind.

At the moment I didn't really care. I had no hope of keeping my activities secret anyway. I drove up the Acequia Madre toward Cristo Rey church. The Acequia Madre is the Mother Ditch; formerly, I have been told, the main water supply of the town. Although hemmed in by modern cement walls as a precaution against floods, it looks very much like a mountain creek that has lost its way and strayed into the big city. Near the center of Santa Fe it disappears underground in several places, but farther upstream it runs openly through a residential district that, like many such, is populated half by Spanish-Americans, and half by Anglos of artistic pretensions—Anglo, in case you didn't know, is the local term for us foreigners who can't speak Spanish.

Anyway, the ditch or stream is the Acequia Madre, and the road along it is also called Acequia Madre, and the address that interested me was a certain number along that road. It had a red door. I don't know why, but a red front door seems to indicate an artistic female just as surely as a red light is supposed to advertise another type of female. All women of my acquaintance who learn the difference between a palette and a pincushion immediately march out and paint their front doors red. Ruth DeVry's front door, for instance, is a deep, rich tone midway between scarlet and maroon.

Having the door spotted, I cruised around the neighborhood in a fashion I hoped looked casual, although it didn't really matter. The Pontiac made the proper negligent attitude hard to achieve; if cars get much bigger, Santa Fe is going to have to close up shop. It's an old city that likes its privacy, which means that every citizen surrounds his property with high adobe walls. These walls, being directly on the street, naturally limit the width of the thoroughfare. The wheelbase and overhang of my vehicle made some of the corners almost impossible to negotiate. I extricated myself from this rabbit-warren at last, and drove back to the hotel for lunch.

After lunch I went up to my room, refreshed my memory from the telephone book, and picked up the phone. The operator got the number for me right away. A girl's voice answered.

"Miss Rasmussen?" I said. "Miss Rasmussen, this is Jim Gregory . . . Gregory. Yes, that's right: Dr. Gregory, the guy you tried to shoot once. I know you don't particularly want to see me," I said, "but I wondered if you'd let me drop around, anyway. . . . Yes, after dinner would be fine. Thank you, Miss Rasmussen."

I hung up and looked at my face in the mirror. It was obviously the face of a man wondering what the hell he was letting himself in for. . . .

Driving over after dinner, I had for a moment the free and light and somewhat guilty feeling of a kid playing hooky: I had no wife and no job and I was on my way to call on a pretty girl. It was an odd and somewhat disquieting illusion. I suppose every man every now and then wishes for a chance to start all over again; not so much that he's dissatisfied with what he's made of his life, as that he's curious to see what else he might have done with it. I found a place a block off Acequia Madre where I could leave the overgrown coupé without obstructing traffic, and walked up to the door. Nina Rasmussen must have been waiting for me; she opened the door within a second or two of my knock.

Then we stood facing each other in the doorway, both remembering very clearly the circumstances of our first and only meeting. I saw that she was again wearing one of those wide, flounced, southwestern skirts. The one she had worn to the hospital to kill me had been yellow; this one was red and white, topped by a peasant blouse of

white cotton with small round sleeves and a loose draw-
string neck. Except for a big silver concha belt that must
have set somebody back at least a hundred dollars, she
was wearing no jewelry, which I liked. Too many women
go hog-wild with that Indian silver. She was better-looking
than I remembered; a healthy blonde girl in her middle
twenties. She still wore her hair quite short; it was almost
a boy's haircut. It had grown out enough so I could not
see where she had been hurt by Natalie's pitcher of gladioli.

"Come in, Dr. Gregory," she said. Her voice was different
from what I remembered, low and pleasant, with no over-
tones of hatred or hysteria. "I think you've met my brother
Tony," she said.

The dark boy who had come to the hospital once was
standing by the fireplace, which was one of those small,
round, deep corner jobs that look like beehives. A couple
of piñon logs were burning inside, without benefit of and-
irons. The rest of the room was in keeping with the native
fireplace, low and dark, with the ceiling supported by the
round log rafters that are called *vigas* and add a couple
of thousand dollars to the value of any New Mexico residence. Back east, there's prestige in an old Connecticut
farmhouse. Here, the snob appeal is in a real adobe house
with genuine *vigas*. Tony looked around and gave me a
brief nod without taking his hands out of his pockets.

The girl said, "I'll get my coat, Dr. Gregory. I won't be
a minute."

Nothing had been said about going out, but I saw no
reason to object. The boy had turned back to contemplate
the fire. His uncompromising back said that I had interrupted an argument of which I had probably been the subject. I wandered around the room. There were the usual
local relics scattered around: a couple of beat-up *kachina*
dolls of more authentic origin than you would find in the
ordinary souvenir shops, an old wooden image of a saint
set in a wall niche made for the purpose, some silver and
copper, a nice bowl of the black pottery that comes, I
think, from San Ildefonso, and a couple of the gaudy Jemez pieces that you're supposed to consider vulgar if you're
any kind of an expert—and we're all experts here—but which
I always like, in small doses. There was a lever-action Winchester over the fireplace. There were two large paintings
on the walls, original oils, signed *F. Wild*.

I approached the paintings cautiously, only because the boy was still giving me his back and there was nothing left to look at except some magazines I had already read. Actually the only safe attitude to take toward home-grown art is one of complete disinterest. If they see you looking, they'll almost inevitably ask for your opinion.

"My stepmother," the girl said, coming up behind me. "Frances Wild. She and Dad were killed in an auto accident four years ago. She was supposed to be quite good. That's the pueblo of Taos." I looked respectfully at the stylized design of white cubes piled one on top of the other. Nina Rasmussen indicated the other paintings. "That one is Monument Valley." It was an orange-red pattern of jagged lines. "Well, let's go," the girl said. "We'll be home early, Tony."

Outside it was still, dark, and quite cold. "Drive or walk?" I asked. "My car's just down the street."

"Walk," she said. "That is, if you——"

"I'll make it," I said.

"I just didn't know if you were completely recovered."

"Completely enough," I said. "Tell me, who painted the door red?"

"The door . . . Oh." She laughed. "Why, Frances did, originally. Why do you ask?"

"Just curious."

"I . . . I never liked her very much. So of course I couldn't paint it a different color afterwards. It would have seemed as if I was trying to wipe out . . ." She stopped. "You're a sinister person, Dr. Gregory. Already you have me telling you all about myself."

"That's what I came for," I said. "You and your brother don't look very much alike, except around the mouth and eyes."

"He takes after Mother. She was pure Spanish, a Trujillo." If you've ever been bored by old Virginia families, stay out of New Mexico. They've got it twice as bad. Nina Rasmussen said, "She died when Tony was born. I was six years old."

I said, "Your luck hasn't been very good, has it? People keep dying on you."

She said, "That wasn't a very tactful remark, Dr. Gregory. From you."

I said, "I didn't come here to be tactful. You don't really expect me to be tactful. What does Tony do?"

"He goes to the University. He's just up for the week-end."

"Does he usually come home for the weekend?"

"Not 'usually,' but every now and then."

"Any particular reason this weekend?"

"No," she said. "Why do you ask?"

"Did he let you know he was coming?"

"No," she said. "Dr. Gregory—"

"He came up to tell you not to have anything to do with me, didn't he?" I said. "I kind of expected that he might. I kind of stalled around to give him time to get here."

She said stiffly, "Dr. Gregory, I don't know what you're driving at, but I don't think I'll answer any more questions. You can take me home now."

I said, "You don't look like a fool, Spanish. Don't act like one."

She stopped, and turned to face me in the darkness. "I don't think I like—"

"Does it matter what you like, Spanish?" I asked. "Why did you agree to see me? You didn't like that; you couldn't have, considering that I shot and killed your boy-friend last fall. Yet you were just as sweet as sugar to me over the phone. Why? What are you scared of, Spanish?"

She said angrily, "Don't call me—"

"I'll call you anything I damn well please," I said. "And you'll take it smiling. And we both know why. We both know that the guy I killed last fall was a dirty sneaking murderer who didn't even have the nerve to do his job right. You didn't know it last fall when you came storming to the hospital to avenge him—neither did I, for that matter. But we know it now. Don't we, Spanish? And we know something else, don't we?"

She whispered, "What else do we know?"

I said, "We know that your brother wasn't just along for the ride. He had a loaded gun, too; and if I'd taken another trail that morning I'd have been Tony's pigeon instead of Paul Hagen's. Do you think Tony would have shot any straighter, Spanish? Or would he have got buck fever too?"

She bowed her head so I could not see her face. Presently she whispered, "What are you going to do?"

I did not speak at once. Then I laughed. It was a harsh and ugly sound in the darkness.

Her head came up quickly. "You didn't know!" she gasped. "You didn't know! It was a trick—"

She hit me. I caught her wrists and held her. I don't like to be hit by anybody, even a woman, without hitting back; if they want to deal with the situation on that plane, they can damn well take the consequences.

I said, "Don't do that again, Spanish. Just because I've got a Ph.D. doesn't mean I don't get mad like ordinary people; and you're spotting me damn close to sixty pounds."

She relaxed slowly. I felt the tension go out of her. I released her. She looked down, rubbing her wrists, and said dully, "I didn't say anything."

"You said enough."

"Do the police—"

"They don't figure in this. It's a private venture."

"How did you—"

"When it happened last fall, I was willing to pass it as an accident. Since then, too many other things have happened; it simply had to fit in somewhere."

"The police investigated very thoroughly. They didn't find anything. You can't prove anything, Dr. Gregory. The fact that . . . that you bullied me into betraying myself is not evidence."

I said, "I'm not looking for evidence, Miss Rasmussen. And I want to apologize for my crude behavior. I knew I'd never get anything out of you by being polite. All I want is information. My wife is missing. I'm trying to find her."

"Your wife! What makes you think Tony—"

"The trail begins with Paul Hagen and Tony. Hagen and I had never met, yet he shot me. We agree now it wasn't an accident. Since he didn't know me, he could have had nothing personal against me. It follows that he must simply have been obeying orders. I'm gambling that the people who've got my wife—whether she went with them voluntarily or otherwise, there's some doubt—were also obeying orders, from the same source. If I can find the man who ordered me killed, I'll have the man who's got Natalie. Does that make sense?"

She said, "You make it sound like . . . like a kind of mad conspiracy!"

"Mad is the word, kid," I said.

"I don't know whether to believe you or not," she said. "If Mrs. Gregory is actually missing, why aren't the police and F.B.I. looking for her?"

"They're looking," I said. "But they're operating on a somewhat different basic theory. They think she's in hiding. I think she's been kidnaped. How did you learn the truth about Hagen and your brother? Did Tony break down and tell you?"

She hesitated. After a while she nodded. "He couldn't keep it to himself, particularly after . . . after I'd made such a fool of myself at the hospital. I didn't believe him at first. Deliberate, cold-blooded murder! Why would they do a thing like that, Dr. Gregory? Why?"

"That's what I was hoping to learn from you."

She shook her head quickly. "He wouldn't say. All he said was that . . . that you had to die. I couldn't get him to explain."

"Will you let me talk to him?"

"I can't stop you," she said. "But if you'll wait and let me explain to him what you want. . . . It's not a trick, is it, Dr. Gregory? You're not just trying to get evidence against him to take to the police?"

I said, "If I got a kick out of turning people over to the police, you'd be behind bars right now, Miss Rasmussen."

"Yes," she said quietly. "I'm remembering that."

I said, "I'll call you in the morning."

She looked at me for a moment, started to speak, checked herself, turned, and walked away. I watched her go out of sight. She walked like a boy, lightly, but without putting any sex into it at all. I looked around, got my bearings, and made my way back to the car.

He must have been crouching behind the spare tire, which, in that model, has been brought back into the open and wrapped in tin just as it was on the cars in which I first learned to drive. That's called modern design. I don't know whether I heard him or caught the shadowy movement out of the corner of my eyes as I was putting the key into the lock; all I knew was that it was time to hit the dirt, gabardine suit or no gabardine suit. As I dropped, I felt the tug at the back of my coat and the thin, cold, painless sensations of a razor-edged blade parting the skin.

I struck the ground and rolled, knowing that he was hovering above me like a hunting hawk, looking for an opening; I reversed myself suddenly, rolled against him, brought him down on top of me, and kicked myself clear. Then I was on my feet, and he was coming up. I kicked him in the face—it was like dealing with a snake; I didn't dare get close enough to use my hands. He went over and rolled away and it was my turn to stalk after him, waiting for a chance; but I hadn't jarred him loose from the knife, and I couldn't see how to close in without letting him use it again. He cut at my legs. I jumped back, and he got his feet under him and crouched there. The knife was a splinter of light in the darkness. He swore at me in Spanish, which is a good language for the purpose.

I thought of the .270 and the three boxes of shells locked up with my camping gear in the trunk of the car. To hell with the shells; all I needed was the gun. It would have been a pleasure to use the butt on him. There was nothing to be gained by running; he was younger than I and had not spent most of the past few months in a hospital bed. Besides, I didn't want to run. If you spend enough time outdoors with a gun in your hands, you establish a certain picture of yourself in your own mind: the picture of a guy who can take care of himself. It may be a childish ideal; it may even be a fake; but you don't betray it by running from a hopped-up kid with a switchblade knife.

I reached slowly into my pants and brought out my pocket knife. It was the boy-scout pattern with screw-driver, leather-punch, and can-opener. The cutting blade is about two and a half inches long. I opened it without taking my eyes off the boy in front of me.

"Antonio," I said softly. "Killer Rasmussen."

I started moving forward. He hesitated, and started moving back. He did some weaving and feinting. I paid no attention. We shuffled slowly along in a curious kind of rhythm. His black hair was hanging into his eyes. His nose was bleeding from my kick and the blood was dripping from his chin. He reached the Pontiac and began sliding sideways along it. I had put it where the angle between two walls made enough of a pull-out to get it off the street; he sidled along the door and fender and reached the adobe wall and the end of the line. I could feel blood warm and wet all down my back.

"What's the matter, Killer?" I whispered. "You want me to turn my back again, is that it?"

He made a sound in his throat and lunged. I watched a fencing match once, in college. The thing I noted particularly was that in the épée bouts, where the target is any part of the body, the good ones did not pay much attention to the torso. They made their points off the other man's sword-arm; after all, it was closer. I watched the knife come driving at me; when it was within range, I reached in past it and cut, at the same time stepping forward and aside to meet his body with hip and shoulder.

The shock was considerable for a recent invalid; but I managed to keep my feet. His head was at my shoulder; I slammed my knife-hand at it, using the hilt for brass knuckles since I couldn't twist around to get the blade into action. I had him pinned between me and the fender of the car. He was making a lot of noise. I hammered his head again, my left hand groping for his right, not knowing whether it was still armed or not. I turned and slammed a knee into him, butted him in the face, slugged him in the stomach, and remembered that I had a knife. I stepped back to see where to put it. Deprived of my support, he fell to the ground. The switchblade knife was lying six feet away. I walked up to him stiffly, and toyed with the notion of slitting his throat. At the moment, the idea seemed to have a lot of merit. . . .

The red front door was locked when we reached it. I worked the knocker, which was shaped like a horseshoe, I guess for good luck. I used it and got no response. It did not seem to be working very well, either as a knocker or as a good luck charm. After about thirty seconds of waiting, I tried the latch. It gave. I pushed the door open, got a fresh grip on the boy, and hauled him inside. There was light in the living room; and light also down the hall to the left.

"Tony?" the girl's voice called, from that direction. "Who's there? *Tony?*"

I dragged my burden that way. We met in the bedroom doorway. Nina Rasmussen had next to no clothes on. She gave a little gasp, and grabbed a dress from the back of a chair. Sometimes her reactions were very naïve and corny. I had been married too long to go into a frenzy at the mere sight of a female without a dress on. She backed away still farther as I came across the room. I reached the bed and dumped my silent companion upon it.

"I took one jerk away from you," I said. "Now I'm giving you one back, which makes us even. Here's his knife, in case he wants to try again."

I tossed the weapon at her feet, and got out of there.

TWELVE

I KILLED HIM three times in my sleep. I tore his throat out, cut his heart out, and opened him up from crotch to breast-bone. Maybe I was regretting lost opportunities. It wasn't a restful night. In the morning I got up and cleaned up the bathroom, where I had made a gory mess patching myself clumsily with the little first-aid kit I keep in the car, after first sneaking into the hotel by a side door. I rolled up the clothes I had been wearing and locked them in my suitcase so they wouldn't scare the maid when she came in to make the bed. I shaved, put on slacks and a loose wool shirt, and went to breakfast in the dining room, a low, wide-open room with lots of tables, pleasant enough, but without the character of the bar. I ordered eggs, orange juice, toast, and coffee from a girl in Mexican costume. She went away. I leaned back to wait and straightened up again; I should have gone to a drugstore and sat on a backless stool.

A shadow fell on the table, and a voice I recognized said, "Good morning, Dr. Gregory. You're up early."

"That makes two of us," I said. "Sit down, Van."

He looked down at me for a moment longer. "You're looking well," he said. "Congratulations on a complete recovery." He made as if to slap me on the back.

I said, "If you've got any use for that hand, better take it away before I bite it off at the elbow."

He withdrew the hand and laughed, pulled out a chair and sat down. "For a theoretical scientist, you have a practical knack of surviving some very awkward situations, Dr. Gregory."

"Uh-huh," I said. "And where the hell were you, may I ask?"

"Not there," he said. "The report only reached me around midnight."

"And your men?" I said. "All paralyzed?"

"One man," he said. "How big a staff do you think I maintain on the appropriation they give us? And how many bright and well-trained young men are attracted by the salaries we can afford to pay? When they do have training it usually isn't police training. Maybe you're lucky he didn't try to intervene, considering the vague notion most of them have of handling a gun. After all, it's not supposed to be a shooting job; we're supposed to get help when we want somebody arrested." Van Horn grimaced. "Anyway, he was watching you, not the car; he had no way of knowing the boy was lying in wait for you there. Before he could act, you had the situation well in hand."

I leaned back cautiously, so the girl in the Mexican costume could set the table. "Had breakfast?" I asked. "Well, how about a cup of coffee?"

"I'll have coffee," he agreed. The girl went away. He said, "Do you mind telling me what you're trying to do up here? Besides get yourself killed, I mean."

I said, "What makes it any of your damn business, Van? I've been suspended from my job; that lets me out as far as you're concerned."

"No," he said, "it doesn't. You've still got information in your head that certain people would give a great deal for. Come on back to Albuquerque and settle down where I can keep an eye on you."

I said, "You go to hell." I grinned at him. We had always understood each other, in a subtle sort of way; at least enough that we didn't have to be polite to each other. "You can't have it both ways, Van. When the Government of the United States decides that I'm trustworthy enough to be paid a salary again, I'll think about taking orders from its hired hands even when they aren't directly my superiors. In the meantime I'm an unreliable sonofabitch without a string on me. So run along and stop pushing free citizens around."

He said, "You know perfectly well that your suspension wasn't meant as a reflection upon your personal—"

"It may not be a reflection on my character, but it sure as hell puts a crimp in my income. What do you want for nothing?"

He said, "I don't want you to disappear to turn up with your head blown off or a knife in your back."

I said, "I've been taking care of myself with fair success and no help from you. What are you going to do if I come back to Albuquerque, sleep at the foot of my bed like a police dog? If somebody wants me dead, and can find somebody with a little guts and brains to do the job, I'll be dead, here or in Albuquerque. If he can't produce any better homicidal talent than I've met so far, I'm reasonably safe anywhere. In any case, there's no indication that anybody's interested in picking my brains with anything more delicate than a .30-30 bullet. And, to put it very bluntly, what the hell's the difference to you and the Project whether I'm alive or dead? You're not using me anyway."

He looked at me for a moment, and looked down at his fingers, busy filling his pipe. "I'm sorry you feel that way," he said.

"I don't feel that way," I said. "I've only worked for the government for slightly more than a third of my total life. I don't expect them to have developed any faith in my loyalty and discretion in that brief space of time. After all, it's only twelve years."

He said, "Dr. Gregory—"

"Don't give me that line about protecting me from having to make a terrible choice," I said. "I know what's expected of me if somebody calls up and offers to trade me Natalie's life for certain documents or figures. It's something we all live with; and it's something against which you can't protect us, because they don't have to telegraph their punch with a stupid kidnaping to do it. All it takes is a phone call, or maybe an envelope with a candid photograph inside, and a hint to the effect that a gun could take the place of the camera. I don't guarantee that I'd react the way you'd want me to; but that's something you can't tell about anybody, since it's something no man can tell about himself. But that's not what you're worrying about, is it? Because you don't really think she's been kidnaped. What you're worrying about is the possibility that my wife herself should call me up and in dulcet tones ask me to join her in Mexico or Nicaragua or Hong Kong or Vladivostok—with the contents of the laboratory safe." I looked at him without affection. "Go home, Van. Stop bothering me. There was a time when I thought you were a pretty good guy for what you are. All security agents are pests; but for a pest you weren't half bad. You seemed to figure that your job was protecting secret information instead of censoring people's consciences, which was a refreshing approach after some security characters I've met. But I guess I overestimated you. After all, your job is to judge people; and if that's the way you judge me, you're a flop. Get out of here and let me eat my breakfast in peace."

He was a funny guy; when I looked at him, his face was

quite pale, but his ears were red. He looked down at the loaded pipe in his hand, and put it away in his coat pocket without lighting it. Then he put the pouch away. Then he picked up his hat from a near-by chair and got to his feet, started to say something, thought better of it, and walked away. I almost felt like calling him back and apologizing for being mean to him—almost, but not quite. I finished my meal, paid for it and the extra cup of coffee, left a quarter tip, and went out to the drugstore near by on the Plaza.

The morning air was cold and the sky was cloudy. There were the usual Indians on the street with long black hair tied around with red or blue ribbons that did not make them look at all effeminate; there were the usual old men sitting on the benches in the park-like center of the Plaza. They would sit there all day. Maybe they sat there all night; I had never checked. I went back to my room with my purchases. When I came in, Nina Rasmussen was sitting on the bed facing the door.

I stopped and looked at her. She was wearing an honest-to-God dress for a change; a plain, blue, zip-down-the-front style with no local color. She was wearing stockings and dark pumps with high heels; the girl was dressed fit to kill. It wasn't a happy thought. There was a purse in her lap. She was holding it tightly.

I said, "Okay. I give up." I turned slowly to close the door; then, with my back to her, lifted my hands and placed them against the panels, somewhat hampered by the package I was holding. "You can do it," I said. "A steady hand, a clear eye, and a little courage, is all it takes. Right between the shoulder blades now. I'll hold still for you."

"Dr. Gregory, please!"

I turned slowly back to face her. "Please what?"

"Please don't," she said. "Don't joke about it!"

"Who's joking?" I said. "How the hell do I know what you've got in that purse?"

She looked down, seemingly startled, pulled the purse open, and dumped the contents heedlessly on the bed, revealing no object larger than a thin wallet and a silver compact. "Are you satisfied?" she asked. "Or do you want to search me?"

"What's the matter?" I said. "Didn't the police ever give you back the .22 pistol? Well, you could have used Junior's knife, or don't you like to get your fingers bloody?" I walked past her to the dresser and ripped open the drugstore package which contained some tape, a box of sterile gauze pads, and a bottle of tincture of merthiolate. I said, "I'm sorry, Spanish. I'm in a nasty mood this morning."

"You have every reason to be," she said quietly. "What are you going to do, Dr. Gregory?"

"You keep asking me what I'm going to do."

"Well, what are you? About Tony?"

"Don't worry," I said. "He's not in jail, is he? Just keep him away from me, and he'll be all right."

"All right!" Her breath caught. "After the way you . . . Granted that you were justified in defending yourself, Dr. Gregory, did you have to be so . . . so brutal? After all, you're a fairly big man, and he's only a boy!"

I turned on my feet to stare at her. "Spanish," I said slowly, "for sheer cold unmitigated gall, you take the prize. This is the second time you've had the nerve to come into my room uninvited to complain about my behavior on the occasion of one of your friends or relations trying to kill me. Miss Rasmussen, did anybody ever try to kill you? Did you ever lie on the ground with a bullet in your guts, wondering if you were dying or crippled for life, while some crazy punk sprayed lead all around you? Did you ever step peacefully up to unlock your car and have a two-bit squirt try to slip five inches of steel into your back?" I filled my lungs with air and blew it out again. "I'm not hardened to it, Spanish," I said softly. "You see, I never went to war. I'm not used to people trying to kill me. I spend most of my time at quiet, intellectual pursuits. I wear my pants shiny behind a desk eleven months out of the year, except for an occasional stroll through a laboratory. I'm a big brain, precious; an egghead if you like. Occasionally, come fall, I get out in the open and fire off a gun and pretend I'm Dan'l Boone, but it's just pretending. I don't expect to meet any wild Indians and I don't expect the deer to shoot back. I don't go out to take any big risks, and when somebody tries to kill me, it upsets me. It makes me mad, even. I don't want to lie dead up in the Jemez Mountians with your boy-friend's bullet in my back; or in a Santa Fe street with your brother's knife between my ribs. I don't want to lie dead anywhere. I know that's unreasonable of me, but then I'm an unreasonable sort of a guy. I'm so damn unreasonable that since you're here I'm going to make you help me with these bandages, since your brother chose to slice me open in a place only a contortionist could reach. Here, catch."

I tossed the stuff into her lap and began to unfasten my shirt. After a moment she rose and went into the bathroom. When I came in, she was washing her hands thoroughly. She shook them dry, rather than use a towel that might have germs on it.

"I'm sorry," she said. "I don't blame you for losing your temper. It was a stupid thing for me to say. Turn around." I did so, and heard her gasp. "You shouldn't have used a handkerchief!"

I said, "I was fresh out of Bandaids eight inches across. You sound like you know something about it."

"I took some nurse's aid training a couple of years ago. Well, it's kind of pointless to keep it sterile now. I'll just trim around it and cover it with a dressing. Have you got a pair of scissors?"

"In my shaving kit." After a while, as she worked back there, I asked, "How's Tony this morning?"

"He'll be all right. He's got an ugly slash along the arm, but no tendons or major blood vessels were damaged, so I . . . I took care of him myself, without calling a doctor."

"I suppose you kind of brought him up," I said.

"Kind of." Her fingers smoothed tape into place on my back, one strip after another. "You really should have some stitches taken, Dr. Gregory, or it'll leave a bad scar."

"It'll have plenty of company," I said. "Some day let me show you where the surgeons played ticktack-toe on my tummy."

"Why didn't you go to a doctor?"

"For the same reason you didn't. A doctor would have had to report to the police."

"You're not going to call them, then?"

I looked at her over my shoulder. "That's what you came here to find out, isn't it?"

"Yes."

"Your own notion," I asked, "or his?"

She hesitated. "His," she admitted. "He wasn't making much sense when I put him to bed. I gave him a sedative. When he woke up, he was in a panic, expecting somebody to drive up and arrest him at any minute. He wanted to run away. I . . . I had to promise to come here and intercede for him."

"You've done it before?"

She frowned. "Done what?"

"Interceded," I said. "Gone to bat for him."

She put a final strip of tape into place, and smoothed it down. "There, that's the best I can do. . . . No," she said, "that's the terrible thing, Dr. Gregory. You probably won't believe it, but this is the first time anything of the sort . . . I don't even know where he got the knife."

I said, "They're easy enough to get; every *pachuco* has one, I understand."

She caught my arm and swung me around to face her. "My brother is no *pachuco*, Dr. Gregory! That's what I'm trying to tell you. He's not a juvenile delinquent; he's never been in any trouble; he got fine grades all through school; and he's doing very well at the University. I'm not saying he's an angel. He drinks and smokes and goes out with girls; and sometimes he undoubtedly drives much too fast, but I've never had any cause to worry about him until—"

"Until last fall," I said.

She nodded. "Yes."

I said, "If he's really a good kid, as you say, once he gets over feeling scared and sorry for himself, he may realize that it could have been worse. He could have waked up a murderer. Maybe the thought will help me persuade him to talk to me; particularly when he learns I'm not going to have him arrested. How about it?"

She hesitated; then she said, "All right. I've pretty well got to trust you, haven't I? And if we can learn what's behind all this, maybe . . . maybe we can help him."

Driving was kind of tricky; it was the first time I had really appreciated all those power gadgets that let me control the car without exerting enough force to push me back against the seat. I pulled up in front of the house; she let us in with her key. I saw her pause; then she was running across the living room, leaving me standing there looking at the pieces of the black San Ildefonso bowl that I had noticed the evening before, now shattered on the floor.

THIRTEEN

TEN MINUTES LATER we had been all over the house, and had also checked the patio and the garage out back. There were no dead bodies on the property. There were a few spots of gore in the bathroom, but it was old gore that she had overlooked while cleaning up last night. Clothes were missing, she said, the boy's jalopy was missing, and sixty-three bucks that had been in the black bowl—household money, she said—was also missing. We decided that the bowl must have slipped out of his weakened hand while he was emptying it; there was no other sign of violence. We decided that there was really nothing to get excited about after all, and went into the kitchen to make coffee, and came out into the living room to drink it.

"Cream and sugar, Dr. Gregory?" she asked.

"Thanks," I said, seating myself on the sofa and accepting the cup she passed across the low table, a heavily constructed piece of smoky-looking old wood that undoubtedly started its career as something other than a cocktail table. She poured her own coffee, and stood there for a moment sipping it black, as if checking whether it was fit to drink. The straight, tailored blue dress, open at the throat, caused me to revise some of my previous doubtful estimates of her figure; and the heels and stockings improved my already favorable opinion of her legs. In civilized clothes she was a very nice-looking girl.

I said, "Okay, Spanish. Where's he gone?"

She spilled some coffee down her chin and had to grab for a napkin to mop herself off. She did not look at me. "What do you mean? I suppose he's just gone back to Albuquerque . . . to the University. Where else would he go?"

"Uh-huh," I said. "And he suddenly remembered he was late for class and dashed out grabbing a handful of bills, in too much of a hurry to sweep up the pieces of the bowl he dropped." I shook my head. "It won't wash."

"Maybe not," she said. "All right; I don't know where he's gone."

I said, "You're a pretty liar, Spanish, but not a very good one."

She looked at me angrily. "I wish you wouldn't call me—"

"What's the matter, are you sensitive about it?"

"No, but—"

I got up and walked around the table to face her. "Where's he gone?"

"I don't know."

I said, "When you first came in, and found him missing, you almost fainted. After all, he'd promised not to run out if you went over and talked to me, hadn't he? You told me that yourself. Then we looked around a little; then you relaxed and became all smiles and hospitality and treated me to the longest and slowest cup of coffee in the history of the bean. . . . He left a message, didn't he? And you found it. And it seemed like a good idea to keep me here as long as possible to give him a head start. Well, are you going to tell me where he's headed, or would you rather tell the police?"

"The police!"

"You're damn right, the police," I said crudely.

"But you said—"

"I said I wasn't going to. That was before he disappeared. Now I'm going to. Where's the phone?"

She cried, "But you can't. . . . What are you going to tell them?"

"That your brother's running amok with a knife and had better be taken into custody before he hurts somebody else."

She stared at me. "But that's perfectly ridiculous! Just because he—" She checked herself.

"Merely because he tried to murder me last night?" I asked dryly. "No, Spanish, I am trying to overlook that insignificant incident. Despite the fact that he tried to murder me last night, I'm trying to save his life."

"His life!" For a moment she looked frightened; then she drew herself up. "Isn't that just a little hypocritical, Dr. Gregory? I suppose you have a right to have him arrested, but you don't really have to pretend you're doing it for his own good! There isn't the slightest indication that his life's in any danger—except from you! Everything shows that he left this house of his own free will—"

"Sure," I said. "And do you know how many other people

mixed up in this have left their houses of their own free wills in the past eight months, and never come back?"

"What do you mean?"

"About eight months ago," I said, "early last summer, an old guy named Fischer who worked in Washington—you've never heard of him, but he was pretty well known in his field—went sailing on Chesapeake Bay of his own free will. He was never seen again. The boat was found drifting, empty. Last fall, an unsavory scientific character named Gregory, whom you've met, went hunting of his own free will. He almost didn't make it back home either. A month or so later a guy named Justin from over at Alamos went skiing up in the Sangre de Cristos of his own free will. He vanished. They didn't even find the skis. A week or so ago an associate of mine named Bates down in Albuquerque got fed up, resigned, and drove up into the mountains to commune with nature. He was found the next morning shot to death with his own gun. A day later my wife decided she'd had enough of one thing and another; she headed for Reno, of her own free will. She never got there. They found the car wrecked but she wasn't around. She still isn't." I paused. "That's just the ones I know. There may be others that security has kept me from hearing about. So when a kid who's obviously involved in the same mess suddenly takes off for parts unknown, I can't take the responsibility of keeping quiet. I've got to get him back to where somebody can keep an eye on him, for his own sake if nothing else."

She studied my face for several seconds after I had finished; then she looked down, seemed to be surprised to discover that she was still holding her cup and saucer, and turned to set them on the tray.

"You're trying to frighten me," she said quietly.

"Sure."

"What . . . what is this thing that you think Tony's got himself involved in? Tony and Paul both."

"I don't know," I said. "Whatever it is, it's big. So big that when somebody told them to go out and kill for it, they went. Would they kill for money, Spanish?"

She started to speak angrily, checked herself, and shook her head. "No," she said. "No, they wouldn't kill for money, Dr. Gregory."

"There are people who would say that communism is a pretty big thing, to those who believe in it."

"My brother isn't a communist, and neither was Paul Hagen!"

"Six months ago you'd have said just as firmly that they weren't murderers. . . . Pass it, Spanish. Don't get mad. I'd say the same about my wife. She's a screwball in many respects, but she's not a communist or a traitor to her country. Yet she's messed up in this too. I want to find her. Tony's my only lead. Even if he knows nothing else, he'll at least be able to tell me why he and Hagen tried to kill me. There's a chance he knows more. Because it's very unlikely that he came up here accidentally this weekend, or even that he just happened to learn somehow that I was coming. It's much more likely that somebody who's been keeping track of my movements saw where I was heading, got hold of Tony, and gave him his orders and a knife. And the reason Tony tried to talk you into not seeing me—I gather that he did from the way both of you were acting last night—is that he didn't really want to kill anybody, and if I didn't come the plan would have to be called off or postponed. But I did come, and he had to make his try, and he missed—maybe he even wanted to miss. That's a pretty shallow groove in my back. Your brother's no better at murder than Hagen was, which I guess isn't really anything against either of them. But now these people, whoever they are, have a failure on their hands; a scared kid, running away, who probably knows too much. All I can say, Spanish, is that if I were running their show, I'd have him wiped out. And if I were you I would let me call the police. They can do more to protect him than we can."

I stopped talking and waited. She looked down at her hands, which were locked tightly in front of her. "I . . . I can't do that. After all that investigation last fall, if he were arrested now he'd never live it down. It would ruin him."

"Sure," I said. "A friend of mine was ruined last week. You should have seen what the buckshot did to him."

She winced. "I'll take you to Tony," she said. "If you'll promise. . . . No. If I can't trust you, you'd break a promise anyway, wouldn't you? Just give me time to change my clothes."

I said, "If we're going out of town, you'd better bring along a sleeping bag or a couple of blankets. I don't like the looks of the weather. And if you've got shells for that thirty-thirty on the wall, we might find room for that, too."

FOURTEEN

NORTH OF SANTA FE you hit some places with really tricky names: Tesuque and Pojoaque, for instance, and, after turning northwest of the Taos road, Abiquiu. This pointed us in the direction of Chama and Brazos. It's rough country up there and high country; to the west is the Jicarilla Apache reservation which, like most Indian reservations, is country no white man was expected to have any use for. That, of course, was back in the days before oil and uranium, but the Jicarillas, unlike their Cherokee and Navajo brethren, are still not getting rich off the grim chunk of wilderness allotted them by a benevolent government. To the east is a solid mass of mountains sliced north and south by various rivers including the Rio Grande, but practically impenetrable in an east-westerly direction. To the north, among other interesting and elevated landmarks, is the ten-thousand-foot Cumbres Pass leading into Colorado.

It's a great country, but it scares the hell out of me. I am, after all, only a part-time pioneer. North of Abiquiu we got rain, which also impaired my morale. Bad weather always worries me west of the Mississippi, particularly between November and May at altitudes over six thousand feet. This was only the end of March; and the gray clouds hung low over the broken landscape as far as you could see —thirty miles and more when the terrain opened up a little, as it did frequently. Ahead, the mountains ran up into the clouds and disappeared.

The road was wet and black in front of us. There were patches of old snow along the hillsides. In ten miles we passed no more than a single pickup truck carrying a load of firewood. The windshield wipers clicked and the heater whined softly and the tires hissed and the miles passed. Nina Rasmussen sat beside me in an alert and ladylike way, her legs neatly crossed and her hands neatly folded in her lap. She was wearing jeans and a black-and-red Mackinaw jacket; she also had a red knitted ski cap and mittens to match,

but she had taken these off after the car had warmed up.
I had changed—when we stopped to pick up my stuff at the
hotel—into my hunting clothes over a firm foundation of
long wool underwear. It may scratch a little, but it can save
your life. In winter, I'd as soon go hunting without my gun
as without the longies. Presently we met another car from
the north. It had snow on the roof and windshield.

I asked, "How much farther?" My voice sounded sudden
and loud after the long silence.

"It's still quite a ways," she said.

"Has Tony got chains on his car? It doesn't look as if he
could get very far off the pavement today without them."

She said, "He's got chains; I hope you have."

"Never fear," I said. "I'm the worrying type. Ever since
I came out to this part of the country, I've been collecting
emergency gear. I've got tire-chains and tow-chains, extra
water and gas, rope, shovel, ax, saw, and a couple of jacks
—did you ever try getting out of a really bad spot with just
one jack? I did, duck hunting along the river a couple of
seasons ago, and went right out afterwards and got another.
We may be short on brains, Spanish, but we're long on
equipment."

We had been driving up a steadily narrowing valley—I
think the valley of the Chama River, but without a map I
wouldn't guarantee that piece of geographical information.
Now the road began to climb away from the river bottom,
first along the side of a hill, and then up a steep and winding canyon. As we gained altitude, we met the first flakes
of snow. They melted off the windshield, but there were
more behind them. I turned the defroster to high and
switched on the lights so that people could see us coming,
as the visibility was getting pretty poor although it was barely
noon. At the top of the canyon, we came out on the level
again, about a thousand feet higher than we had been. Up
here the snow was already beginning to stick to the blacktop
pavement. The surrounding country was white. I pulled out
on the shoulder and stopped the car.

"How much farther now?" I asked, when she looked at
me.

"It's still twenty or thirty miles on this road, I think."

"It would," I said, "be nice if you were sure, Spanish.
What is the place, anyway?"

"Just a spot where we sometimes camp in the summer.
I'll know the turn-off when we come to it."

"How much of a jaunt after that?"

"Another twenty-five miles, more or less."

"Bad road?"

"It's probably pretty bad at this time of year."

I grimaced. "Well, in that case we're bound to need the chains, so we might as well put them on now before the stuff gets knee-deep out there. Let's go." Outside the warm and luxurious car it was a different world, cold and bleak, with the big flakes drifting steadily out of the gray sky. I pulled the trunk open, and glanced at the girl, who was pulling her red hat down over her ears. "Sometimes I wonder what goes on in the minds of those characters in Detroit," I said. "They sell me two hundred horsepower and air conditioning for four thousand bucks. The windows go up and down at the touch of a button. I can put up the radio antenna by wiggling a finger, and move the seat back and forth without exerting more than an ounce of effort. Everything's been done to make life lovely for me—as long as I stay on smooth, dry pavement. But if the road gets a little muddy or a little snow starts to fall, I've got to get out and crawl under the damn car just like my dad did with his Model T. That's progress?"

She laughed, picked up the chains, sorted out one, and draped it over the nearest wheel while I worked with the jack. There are other ways of doing it, but the new cars have the wheels so wrapped up in streamlining you can hardly get at them without jacking up the rear end. Fifteen minutes later we were under way again. With the chains on, we had a noisy couple of miles at first, until the snow built up enough to stop the racket; then we proceeded in a kind of muffled and vibrating silence. There were tracks in the road to show that we were not alone in the universe; occasionally we met a car or truck heading south, but you couldn't call it heavy traffic. This was just as well, since everyone was using the same two ruts in the center of the highway, only pulling out into the fresh snow at the sides to pass.

"Take it easy now," Nina said at last. "I think we're getting close. . . . Yes, there it is. Turn left at the sign."

I stopped at the intersection and got out to look around. It was a small state road heading west. It looked here as if it might have a fair gravel surface under the snow, but I didn't count on that lasting very far. Those small roads usually deteriorate pretty rapidly as you get away from the main highways. Several cars had used it within the past hour or two; the snow had only started to fill in the latest tracks.

"What do you think?" Nina said at my shoulder.

"People have gone that way," I said. "Or come. I'm not a good enough tracker to tell. Two or three cars at least. One jeep, I'd say. What's Tony driving?"

"Well," she said, "I think it started out as a Ford, but the factory wouldn't know it now. He got two new tires recently, but I wouldn't recognize the treads."

I glanced at the sky, and at the surrounding country; a bleak pattern in white and black, without color or intermediate tones of gray. "No sign of this letting up," I said. "We can make it up to Chama, or back to Santa Fe. But if we head over that way, this late in the day, it could get rough."

"You're the one who said he was in danger, Dr. Gregory."

"Sure," I said, "but you're the one who's going to have to spend the night with me if we can't get this glamorbuggy back out of there."

She said, "Aren't you being a little silly and oldfashioned? I'm willing to risk it if you are."

I said, "It's no risk to me, Spanish. I'm not a virgin."

I heard her breath catch at this; and I looked at her directly and appraisingly, just to make it a little tougher. She had not put her cap back on to step out here, and the snow was melting in her hair. The heavy clothing gave her all the lissome grace of a teddy bear. She had a nice, practical, durable look about her.

I always feel that you can tell a lot about a girl by the way she wears jeans. The first criterion is the size and condition of the garments: if they are big and stiff and new, she's a tenderfoot; if they are soft and faded and skin-tight, she's a tramp or a teen-ager working hard at becoming one. The second thing to look for is the treatment she accords the legs. If she turns them up to her calf and beyond in a variety of cute ways, leave her in town. She'll be a menace in camp. If she wears them all the way down to her instep, but still turns up a six-inch cuff, you can give her the benefit of the doubt if you feel charitable. At least she knows enough to protect her shins from the brush and cactus. She may have seen too many cowboy movies, but she may just have got hold of a long pair by accident. But if the pants just fit like pants instead of like some kind of dancing tights;

and if they simply terminate at the ankles without any fancy turn-up, watch yourself, brother. She's been out in the woods long enough to discover that a turned-up pants cuff is nothing but a dirt-catcher and can cost you a broken leg or worse if it happens to hang up on the wrong thing at the wrong time. Nina Rasmussen was wearing a comfortable-looking pair of jeans that stopped just short of her instep without fuss or apology.

She said quietly, "You didn't have to say that."

I said, "Of course I had to. Or something equally crude and convincing. Otherwise you'd have tried to kid yourself that I was some kind of pure and dedicated character, searching for my lost wife like Galahad searching for the Holy Grail. Now, do we go after your brother or do we go back to Santa Fe?"

She laughed. "We go on, Dr. Gregory. And I'll try not to strain your self-control beyond the breaking point, if we should have to spend the night together."

I grinned, and we went back to the car. The next hour we covered ten miles and I never worked harder. The cut on my back made it something less than fun. The snow kept falling implacably and the road got progressively worse and you couldn't tell where the holes were because everything was white. The long, overhanging tail of the Pontiac smacked bottom on the sharper dips; I don't know what fool ever got the idea of building a car out six feet behind the rear wheels. The second hour we made seven miles. We passed a lumber mill with no sign of life around, and saw one distant ranch house. There were no longer fences along the road, or even telephone or power lines. There was only the high plain covered with snow, out of which rugged mesas rose all around us, spotted with snow-laden evergreens and, occasionally, with bare rock too steep to hold the snow.

I asked, "Are you going to know this place when we get there, in this stuff?"

"I think so," she said.

"Is there any kind of shelter around?"

She nodded. "There's an old cabin. . . . Go slow now. I think we turn just ahead. What's the speedometer reading?"

"By your figures, we've got six miles left to go, approximately." As usual, I had noted the reading when we left the main road.

She said, "That's about right. This must be it. Turn right up that canyon."

I said, "First let's take a look," and stopped the car in the middle of the road, where I could hope to get it started again. We got out, and waded over to the culvert that carried the side road over the shallow ditch. I said, "A car with chains has gone up and is still up there. Or, possibly, it was up there and came out after the snow started. A jeep with chains on all four wheels has gone in and come out. We can't have missed it by too much; the tracks are still fresh."

She glanced at me, and we turned quickly and hurried back to the car. I sent it bouncing over the culvert, the rear end struck bottom as usual—it occurred to me that I'd better take a look at the tailpipe at the next opportunity— the hydramatic shifted gears as the road started to climb, and the canyon walls closed in on us. We clattered across a wooden bridge over a good-sized creek flowing clear and brown among snow-covered stones and ice. Presently we were in among the pines.

"It's an old logging road," Nina said. "There are some pretty good trout in the creek."

"I used to fish when I was a kid," I said. "Then my time got too scarce for both hunting and fishing, and I liked hunting better, so I gave my tackle away."

"How far now?" she asked.

"Four and a half by the clock."

"If the jeep came out again, why didn't we meet it on the road?"

"It went on to the west," I said.

"It's fifty miles to the highway, that way."

"They can make it," I said, "in a jeep. You can do anything in a jeep, except make love. Maybe that, too. I wouldn't doubt it's been tried."

She smiled. "You seem suddenly to have sex on your mind, Dr. Gregory."

"What's wrong with sex?" I asked. "It's better than what you've got on your mind, isn't it?"

She was silent. We hit a curve a little too hard. I missed the tracks of the vehicles that had gone before, plowed into fresh drifted snow, and came to a halt with the rear wheels turning futilely. I backed up and tried again, but my own tracks threw me out where I had been. I backed up a second time, a little farther, stepped her all the way down, hit it hard, and made six feet. I backed up a third time, charged the soft barrier again, and gained another six. On the next try she broke through and kept going. We crossed the stream again, and then a third time. I was glad I wasn't in the first car to cross those bridges that afternoon. It occurred to me, however, that I was probably in the heaviest.

There was a wind starting to blow now. Twice I had to back up and take a run at spots where the previous tracks had drifted over—and this was in a sheltered canyon. Out in the open it was going to be a bad night. Already now at a little past three in the afternoon the light was beginning to fade. Nina gave me no warning although she must have known we were getting close. Suddenly we came around a bend and there was the jalopy parked under the trees ahead. I found a spot where I could turn the Pontiac and leave it pointing downhill. There did not seem to be anybody around.

We got out. "Where's the cabin?" I asked.

"Up there through the alders," she said, pointing. "He must have . . ."

She stopped and looked around, frowning. I heard the sound at the same time; the engine of the jalopy was running. We ran through the snow toward it.

"Look!" Nina cried.

A rubber hose ran from one of the twin exhaust pipes alongside the car and up into the rear window, which was open enough to receive it. All other windows were closed. I stepped forward and pulled the right door open. A wave of exhaust gas hit me in the face. There was nobody in the car. I ran around to the other side, Nina stumbling along beside me. The left door was not fully latched, as if it had been opened and allowed to swing shut of its own weight. There were marks in the snow. We followed them up into the trees and found him lying there.

FIFTEEN

THE CABIN WAS a log shanty with a sloping roof, set up at the edge of the pines on higher ground, out of reach of the spring floods that come roaring down all those canyons—and not always in the spring, either. It had a door, a window, a cast-iron stove, and a built-in bunk. The door had no lock and not much in the way of hinges. The window lacked some glass, but black roofing paper had been tacked over the broken panes. The bunk held the remnants of a straw mattress and probably lots of other things as well. The stove was rusty but looked in reasonable shape otherwise, and was the only thing that really mattered as long as the walls stood and the roof did not fall in. We dragged the boy inside and stretched him on the floor. Nina peeled off her Mackinaw and put it over him, and knelt beside him.

I said, "You can look at him later. He's breathing; that's all we need to know right now. Run back and get his clothes out of his car and all the covers you can carry. Then get him out of those wet things and wrap him up good while I see about getting a fire going."

I stood there after she had hurried out, looking down at the kid, not because I cared what he looked like at the moment, but because hauling the heavy end of him three hundred yards through the snow and alders had taken a lot out of me and I needed puffing time. As far as my physical condition was concerned, I had picked a hell of a time to go adventuring. The kid had a funny pink look that made him seem rosy with health at first glance; that would be the result of the carbon monoxide.

When I was in graduate school, one of my fellow-students got depressed one night over the possibility that he might not pass a forthcoming exam, and turned on all the Bunsen burners in one of the small labs without bothering to light them. I saw him when they carried him out dead the next morning; I was one of those summoned hastily from up the hall to help air out the place before it blew up the building. I could remember thinking callously that if I were going to kill myself over an exam, which wasn't likely, I'd at least wait until the damn thing was over and I had been officially informed that I had flunked. . . .

Tony seemed to be breathing fairly regularly. I went over and cleaned out the stove, checked the stove-pipe inside, and then went out and climbed on the roof, cautiously, to check it outside. There was no sense in hauling him all this way just to dose him with more monoxide. On my way to the car for an ax and saw, I met Nina staggering under a load of blankets and duffel bags. We didn't speak; we'd met before.

Half an hour later the cabin was warming up enough so that she looked up in annoyance when my opening the door let in a draft of cold air. I dumped an armload of wood on the growing pile and said, "If you've got him warm, put your coat back on and start bringing in the stuff from the trunk of my car. And there's a pint of whisky in the glove compartment. Bring that, too."

She said, "Dr. Gregory, come here a minute. Look." She lifted the boy's head and touched the rear of it gently and showed me blood on her fingers. "They knocked him out and . . . and put him in the car to die!" she said. "It was supposed to look like suicide! If he hadn't come to and managed to get the door open—"

"Sure," I said. "We'll put a Bandaid on it. Later. Now will you stop mooning over him and do a little work before it gets dark? I want everything out of the trunk except the tools and spare tire; and all your stuff out of the rear seat."

She said sharply, "If you want it, why don't you get it yourself?"

"Spanish," I said, "I would just love to do all the work while you sit and hold his head; unfortunately I spent a month or two in the hospital not so long ago, and while I wouldn't hesitate a moment to work myself to death for you, it might leave you kind of lonely up here."

She looked up at me for a moment; then she picked up her Mackinaw and started for the door, stopped to pull the coat on, and looked back as she fastened it about her.

"I'm sorry, Dr. Gregory," she said. "I haven't been much help. I'm just . . . scared to leave him, I guess. He looks so helpless."

I said, "I'm sorry, too. I get even meaner than usual when I get tired, although it hardly seems possible." She smiled at this, and started to turn away. "Nina," I said.

"Yes?"

"Don't forget the rifles and ammo."

She gave me a quick look, nodded, and went out. I went over to give a couple of licks to the pump of the gasoline lantern that was making the little shack a bright and cheery place, at least in comparison with the howling twilight outside. I looked around for a safe place to hang the thing—any gasoline-burning appliance indoors makes me very nervous. I finally wired it solidly to a nail in one of the rafters. The roof was beginning to leak a little here and there as the heat melted the snow above. There were drafts from various cracks between the logs, but the stove was doing a fine job. For any purpose except romance, a stove is worth fifteen fireplaces.

I stood over the boy for a moment. She had bundled him up well and covered him with blankets. He was still unconscious, but still breathing. If he stopped, we'd have to try artificial respiration, but I had no faith in it. Under the circumstances, he'd pretty well have to make it on his own or not at all. Methylene blue was supposed to help, but we didn't have any. I understand that sometimes they give transfusions, but we didn't have the equipment for that, either. We were even, at this altitude, a little short of the oxygen he badly needed.

"Keep plugging, kid," I said. He didn't hear me. I picked up my ax and went out again. The wind was whipping the snow from the trees now, and sweeping it off the ground, to add to what was already in the air; it was clearly going to be one of those nights when man is just a bug clinging to a rock in a hostile universe. It occurred to me to wonder if Van Horn had had any men following me today. Well, they were his responsibility, not mine. I carried in several more loads of wood; fortunately there was plenty of down timber around. I dragged a couple of logs near the door where I could work on them in the morning. It was getting too dark to be wandering around out there; I almost missed the cabin on the last trip. I went back inside. It would have been a pleasant scene if it had not been for the boy lying on the floor. Nina was setting up the stand for my two-burner gasoline stove in the corner.

"There's coffee on the fire," she said. "The guns are over on the bunk."

"Did you wipe them off?"

"No," she said dryly, "I thought they'd look prettier rusty."

"Sorry," I said. "How's he doing?"

"No change. Dr. Gregory, do you think he . . ." Her voice seemed to fade out for a minute. It was a queer sensation. "Dr. Gregory!" she said sharply. She was standing right in front of me now. I wasn't quite sure how she had got there. "Sit down over here," she said, taking my arm. "I'll bring you some coffee. How about a little whisky in it?"

I nodded, sat down on the bunk, pulled off my cap and gloves and shook the snow off them.

"I'm all right," I said when she came back to me.

"You'd better be," she said, and put an aluminum cup in my hands. "Drink this. If you crack up, I'll just shoot all three of us, Dr. Gregory. I don't want to be a little heroine all by myself."

The hot coffee laced with whisky tasted wonderful. I sipped it and looked up at her. She still looked like a teddy bear in the heavy jacket that she had unbuttoned but had not taken time to remove. Her hair was damp and spiky all over her head; it looked as if she had given it a quick rub with a towel and forgotten about it. Looking at her, I had the odd and rather disturbing feeling of recognition that you sometimes get with a girl. A little voice says: *This one would do.* It doesn't have to mean anything; usually it doesn't. You may be happily married to the woman of your choice. She may be happily married and have five perfect children. It's just a little reminder that life is a series of random occurrences that could have occurred differently.

I said, "Most people call me Greg. Some call me Jim. Take your choice."

She laughed. "Most people call me Nina. May I ask a question?"

"Ask ahead."

"You said your wife was on her way to Reno to divorce you when she disappeared. You even gave the impression that . . . well, that some people think she might have disappeared of her own accord. Well, if that's the case, why not let her go?"

I said, "Because I've got to be sure, Spanish. . . . I mean, Nina. Don't you see? If this is the way she wants it, okay. If she wants to go to Reno, I won't stand in her way. If she wants to disappear, that's her business. But no ringtailed monkey of a two-bit conspirator is going to take my wife anywhere she doesn't want to go, or make her do anything she doesn't want to do. Not as long as she's my wife, he isn't."

"You're a funny person," she said. "You're not at all what I would have expected from the work you do."

I got up and went over to the corner where the food was piled, found the pint flask, and poured a little whisky into my empty cup. I found another cup, poured a little into that, too, and went back to where she was standing and put it into her hands. A gust of wind shook the cabin and blew snow through the crack beneath the door. It set up a low, roaring note in the stove-pipe that lasted for a second or two and died away. Nina tasted the liquor in the cup.

"It doesn't taste like much without ice," she said.

"If ice is what you want," I said, "there's plenty around."

I sat down beside her. It was a very peculiar situation. If it had not been for the boy on the floor, I might have tried to take advantage of it in a polite and gentlemanly way. I certainly won't ask anyone to believe that the idea never crossed my mind. That it had crossed hers, too, was apparent from the little look she gave me, clearly estimating just what she might have to contend with before the night was over.

I said abruptly, "People expect us to live up to our publicity as cold, objective, unemotional men of science, dedicated exclusively to the advancement of human knowledge. It's that way with any art or profession; the guy usually doesn't look at all the way he does in the movies. I had the biggest shock of my life the first time I met an opera singer. I expected some kind of a pansy. He turned out to be a big tough guy who used to work as deckhand on a freighter. His pet parlor trick after he'd had a couple of drinks—and he was a guy who might just take a couple of drinks if you coaxed him—was to lie down on the floor and ask you to jump on his stomach with both feet. Then there's the sensitive artist type we know in Albuquerque, who likes to paint deserts. He strolls around Death Valley in the middle of summer with all his paraphernalia on his back, having a whale of a good time at a hundred and ten in the shade. One day he decided he was just packing too damn much stuff around, and the only thing he didn't need to paint with was the canteen. So now he's trained himself to go all day without water. Just a creampuff, like us highbrow intellectuals." I shook my head. "I was born on a farm in Wisconsin. Nobody thought I was particularly bright until I got to high school; and that it was just a math teacher who helped me get a scholarship to Chicago because I could do cute tricks with numbers in my head, even though I was hard to catch during hunting season and still am. I used to like fishing, too, but not as much, so when my time got limited and I had to choose between them, I kept the guns and let the tackle go."

"I know," she said, smiling. "You told me that, driving up here."

I got to my feet. "Well, it's bad enough to tell a girl the story of your life; but when you start repeating yourself it's really time to quit. . . . Nina."

"Yes," she said, looking up.

"Don't worry about it. I'm lousy with self-control. I even quit smoking once and never went back. You're just as safe as you want to be."

She laughed and rose to face me. "That sounds as if I might not be safe at all."

"I said, "Well, you wouldn't want to think there wasn't a little risk, Spanish. That would take all the fun out of life. Besides, you wouldn't deprive me of the male privilege of acting virile and dangerous, even though I'm so bushed that five minutes from now you're going to have drag me out the door if the place catches fire, since I'll be too sound asleep to wake up for anything."

"I'll do it, too," she promised. "Good night, Jim."

SIXTEEN

IN THE MORNING we had scrambled eggs and bacon washed down with strong coffee, so you would hardly classify it as a hardship case as far as two of us were concerned; and the boy was still with us. Afterwards I went down to the creek for water. The wind was still blowing and the snow was still falling, but weather never looks quite so bad when you know you've got seven or eight hours of daylight ahead of you. The temperature wasn't anything to complain about, either; probably around fifteen or twenty above zero, which in that dry air is no cold at all. You never get really cold weather out there with a cloudy sky. When it clears off is when the mercury can hit twenty below without half trying. But it was late in the season for a real cold snap; and there was hope that this storm might be followed directly by a thaw.

When I returned to the cabin, Nina had the sleeping bags draped over the bunk to air. She had disposed of the rotten straw mattress, probably in the stove, and was sweeping out the place with a little hand whiskbroom I keep in the car, that had got brought in with the rest of the paraphernalia.

"He was awake for a minute," she said. "He recognized me."

"Good," I said.

"If . . . if he lives, I'll be grateful all the rest of my life," she said.

"Sure," I said. "Where the hell's the detergent?" I found the bottle and dumped a capful into the pail I had brought in, set it on the stove to heat and began to scrape the dishes. I heard her laugh. "What's so funny?" I asked.

"Why is it that the easiest way to make a man squirm is to start talking about gratitude? Leave those dishes alone; I'll do them. Come over here and take your shirt off; I'll bet those dressings on your back are a mess by this time." I dropped the dishes into the pail to soak, and went over

105

and peeled to the waist, which took a little doing, what with the stuff I had on. She said, "You're just a big hero, aren't you? Why didn't you say something?"

I asked, "Just what the hell were you going to do about it, kiss it and make it well?"

"Well, hang on now. This is going to hurt."

She pried the tape loose and yanked it off in a nice, brutal, professional way; it takes somebody with hospital training to really get the most out of a hunk of adhesive tape. Then she cleaned things up and taped me again; and went over to throw the old bandages into the stove while I got my clothes back on.

"How does it look out there?" she asked.

"Still coming down. I wouldn't say it had slacked off very much." I glanced at my watch, remembered that I hadn't wound it this morning, and repaired the oversight. "Remind me in about fifteen minutes and I'll go out and try to pick up a nine o'clock weather report on the car radio, although I don't know how much reception I'm going to get down among all this rock. . . ."

I broke off as the boy on the floor began to moan in a distressed way, squirming in his blankets. He spoke the first comprehensible words I had heard out of him since we found him.

"Hurts!" he gasped. "Ah, it hurts. . . ."

"Where, Tony?" she cried, kneeling beside him. "What hurts?"

"My chest. . . ."

There was more, but you couldn't read it. He thrashed around weakly; then curled up in a tight ball, hugging himself. He seemed suddenly to be shaking all over. You could actually hear his teeth chattering. I went over to the bunk and got my sleeping bag, which contains six pounds of Dacron —not quite as warm or as light as down, but a lot less expensive. She had already zipped it fully open to air it. I spread it over the kid like a blanket. She tucked it around him tightly. Presently she rose and looked at me; we moved off together a little distance, the way you do when you are going to talk about a sick person.

"Jim, we've got to get him to a doctor," she said. "I'm not much of a nurse, but my mother died of pneumonia and this looks like the same thing."

I said, "It can't be done, Spanish."

"It's got to be done. He'll die if he doesn't get the proper treatment."

I said, "We'd have to take the car, to keep him warm. Making a toboggan of sorts and hauling him would probably be easier, but he couldn't stand it. And we've got six solid miles of snow down the canyon; and there's no assurance they'll have put a blade over the state road when we get there—if we get there. They don't usually plow those little roads until they've got the main highways clear, and that'll probably keep them busy all of today. So it adds up to a possible twenty-five miles of shoveling to reach the highway. And I simply haven't got the strength for it. Not even six miles of it. There's no use kidding ourselves. I couldn't do it. I'm sorry."

She said, "I can use a shovel."

I said, "Sure. You're a big husky girl and you can carry the damn car through the drifts on your back." I shook my head. "Let's face the facts. If we get a couple of miles down the road and poop out, we're worse off than if we'd never started. *He's* worse off." After a moment I said, "Even if it is pneumonia, people have lived through it."

"Not in a place like this. Not after being poisoned by exhaust gas."

I said, "We aren't taking him out, Spanish. Not the two of us, by ourselves. Because we couldn't make it. There's an alternative, however. If you can hold the fort, I'll go out on foot and get some help."

She hesitated, and studied my face. "It's a long way. If the storm should get worse again you might . . . might have trouble."

I said, "Hell, legally it's spring even if the weather doesn't seem to have heard about it. This thing won't last much longer. But it's apt to take me a little time. If there's nobody on the road, I'll have to hoof it to that ranch we passed about fourteen miles back. Say I do two miles per hour; that's seven hours. Then I'll have to round up some equipment and get back here. There's not much chance of my making it before dark. Think you'll be all right?"

She nodded. "I'll be all right. But maybe I should go. I haven't been sick like you. I'm in good shape."

I grinned. "You certainly are, Spanish. I've been admiring your shape for quite a while." I stopped grinning, and said, "No. You know more about taking care of him than

I do. Well, make me up a couple of sandwiches, will you, while I get some stuff together?"

I got my compass, hunting knife, waterproof match safe, drinking cup, and a small flashlight out of my hunting kit; then I picked up the .270 and shoved five shells into the magazine, closed the bolt on the empty chamber, and adjusted the sling so the gun would hang easily from my shoulder. I dropped a handful of extra cartridges into my pocket.

"What's that for?" Nina asked, coming up with a paper bag in one hand and a cup of coffee in the other. "The gun, I mean."

"I wouldn't feel natural, walking around the mountains without a gun."

"That's silly," she said. "It's seven or eight pounds more weight to carry. There's nothing in these mountains that'll hurt you."

I glanced at the sick boy, and said, "You've got a short memory, Spanish. I might meet a jeep. I always wanted a nice stuffed jeep head over the mantelpiece. You'd better load up that thirty-thirty when I'm gone." I pocketed the sandwiches, drank the coffee, and gave the cup back. "Well, be good," I said, and went out.

The wind was still blowing, but it was coming down the canyon so I had it with me. The visibility wasn't as bad as it had been the day before. I passed the cars; snow had drifted up against them until you could hardly see them from windward. I was glad I had plenty of anti-freeze in the Pontiac. Then I was in the timber again and there was nothing to remind me of the place except a whiff of wood-smoke carried by the wind.

It took me an hour to reach the first bridge, which was no better than par for the course. The hour entitled me to five minutes' rest—if you don't put yourself on some kind of schedule, you'll find yourself sitting on every stump along the road—so I set the gun against a tree and went down to the creek for water. It was hard to get at for the ice along the bank, but I managed to crack this without getting wet. The water was too cold to drink fast. I squatted on the bank, sipping it cautiously and listening to the noise of the creek and thinking about nothing in particular except the various aches that were developing in my thighs from lifting each foot out of one hole in the snow and setting it down in another a small distance ahead.

Then I heard a sound. It was no more than a break in

the rippling sound of the creek; I could not identify it. I got up slowly; after you've hunted a while, you get out of the habit of making quick motions. I emptied the cup, collapsed it, put it back into its case, and dropped it into my pocket, listening all the while. I moved deliberately back to the rifle and picked it up, but did not sling it on my shoulder. I listened some more. Then I pulled the bolt out of the gun and looked down the bore to make sure no snow had blocked the muzzle. I replaced the bolt, feeding the top cartridge from the magazine to the chamber. I set the safety and put my gloves back on.

I waited a while longer. Nothing happened. My heart started beating normally again. I shrugged, and started down the road; and stopped abruptly, hearing, from ahead, three faint shots in rapid succession, the universal wilderness cry for help.

SEVENTEEN

THERE WERE TWO of them. Their scoutmaster would have been proud of them; they had managed to build a fire in the lee of a big granite boulder. They weren't dressed for the country or the weather. They seemed to be wearing ordinary low shoes, and pants that had probably been nicely creased yesterday but were frozen shapeless about their legs today. The taller of the two was wearing one of those green waist-length airforce jackets that are warm enough as far as they go but leave the seat of your pants hanging out to freeze. He had either come out without a hat or it had blown away; he had a white handkerchief tied about his head like a bandage, covering his ears.

The shorter man was wearing a light topcoat, and a Stetson that I thought looked familiar. As I came closer, I recognized the amiable features of Paul Edward Van Horn, bearded, and blue with cold. Both men were cold and tired enough to have little interest in looking around them, particularly if it involved facing the wind, and the snow that had ceased falling in big flakes and was now coming down in small, hard grains that, windborne, seemed to have a cutting edge. I was almost on top of them before they saw me.

"Hi, Van," I said, stopping by the fire.

He said, "Well, I'm glad to see you alive, Dr. Gregory. We've been looking for you."

"Who's shooting at what?" I asked.

"We weren't quite sure you'd come this way; the tracks were pretty well drifted over when we started up in here last night. As a matter of fact we were about to turn back, but decided to stop and thaw out a little first. I just fired a few shots in case you might be somewhere within hearing."

"Where's your car?"

"About three miles back, stuck tight. We didn't have chains, only snow tires. We spent the night there. The engine quit around three this morning. It got a little chilly after that."

I said, "If you didn't follow people around, you wouldn't

110

get into trouble. Well, we've got a sick man a couple of miles up the canyon. How are you boys with shovels?"

"A sick man? Who?"

"Give your profession a rest, Van. We've also got a nice warm cabin and plenty of food. You can ask the questions when we get there."

Uphill and against the wind, it took considerably longer to go back than it had to come down. When we got there, the cabin was still where I had left it, and smoke was still coming from the stove-pipe. The tall young fellow, whose name I never learned, was pretty cold and miserable: he started running clumsily when he saw it, like a thirsting man heading for an oasis. I called him back.

"Whoa, there," I said. "Just hold it a minute. She's got a loaded Winchester in there, and she isn't expecting me back before dark." I took the .270 off my shoulder, worked the bolt, aimed at the sky, and pulled the trigger. Even in the wind and snow, the big gun crashed loudly enough to hurt your ears. "Yo, Spanish!" I shouted. "Reinforcements coming in."

There was a little pause. I had time for a sickening sense of apprehension; time to know that the door wasn't going to open, that we were going to go inside and find something terrible—or, worse, nothing at all. Other people had turned up missing in more civilized places than this. I shouldn't have left her here with only a sick and helpless kid for company. . . . Then the door swung open, and she looked out at us with the carbine over her arm. Van and his companion started forward again. I paused to throw the empty out of my rifle, and unload. There were plenty of firearms around if we should need them, and I was taught never to bring a loaded gun into the house.

I looked up to see her coming down the path toward me, half running. She stopped in front of me, a little out of breath. She was bareheaded and kind of tousled-looking, and a light application of lipstick wouldn't have ruined her appearance, but you operate on somewhat different standards of personal cleanliness and adornment when you get out into the back country in winter. She looked all right to me.

"Are you all right?" she asked. "I was kind of worried about you."

"Sure," I said. "How's Tony?"

"He's starting to cough. It sounds as if he'll tear himself apart inside."

"Well, as soon as everybody gets warmed and fed, we'll have him out of here." I slung the empty rifle on my shoulder. "I'll go make sure the car's going to start while you see that our guests are well supplied with energy-building foods." I started to turn away.

"Jim," she said.

I turned back. "Yes?"

We faced each other for a moment. Suddenly she was in my arms and I was kissing her with the snow blowing around us and the two rifles getting mixed up together—I remember hoping vaguely that the hammer of the carbine wasn't cocked. It was an odd experience on all counts. I had not had any girl but Natalie in my arms for better than three years; and I'd never had a great deal of time for girls before that, so I wasn't quite sure what was expected of me. We had too many clothes on for any serious display of affection; it was a very innocent kiss. At last Nina turned her face aside and buried it in the damp fur of my hunting-coat collar. I said, "I don't know what the hell I'm going to do with you, Spanish. At the moment, I've already got one wife."

"I know." Her voice was muffled. Presently she straightened up, stepped back, and put her hands to her hair, pushing it back from her face against the wind. "I know. I just . . . if anything had happened to you, after I'd sent you out in all that snow and wind, I'd have died, Jim!"

I looked at her for a moment longer; and she looked back at me steadily. It was like coming to an unmarked fork in a trail. I could not quite see which was the proper direction to take. Well, it did not have to be decided in the middle of a blizzard.

"This could develop into quite a problem," I said. "Let's shelve it temporarily, shall we?"

She laughed quickly. "You're a funny person. Don't be so farsighted, my dear; it doesn't pay. Maybe I just kissed you because I was glad to see you. Maybe I just go around kissing all sorts of men. There's no problem unless . . . unless you want to make one."

"I know," I said. "That's just the problem, whether to make a problem or not. Well, let's pass it for the time being. Tell those guys to hurry up and eat while I see just how big a job we're going to have getting out of here."

The rear of the Pontiac was pretty well covered with snow. I set the rifle aside, took out my heavy hunting knife, and chopped a pine branch to use for a broom—a big hunting knife is generally considered to be the mark of a tenderfoot, but I don't go along with that theory. I've got a pocket knife for fine whittling; I see no point in wearing a toothpick on my belt, too. I pushed and swept the snow off the trunk lid and opened it up. I wiped off the rifle and put it back into its case. Then I got the shovel out and dug around the car, and cleaned off the radiator and windshield. Finally I got inside and started the motor, relieved and pleased to have it start right away. I nursed it along until it was idling smoothly —they've taken the old manual choke and throttle away from us and replaced them with an unpredictable thermostatic gadget, so now you can't warm up a car properly without staying with it every second of the time.

I left it running, climbed out into the snow, and waded over to Tony's car to look for another shovel. They are practically standard equipment for anyone who does much back-road driving in this part of the country, and I found one in the trunk. Then I looked in front to see if Nina had brought out everything of value, since the car might be standing there some time, and the local Indians were probably no less averse to stripping a deserted car than white men would be in similar circumstances. The smell of exhaust gas was still noticeable. There was nothing inside except some magazines on the seat; apparently Tony had stocked up with reading matter before heading for his hide-out.

I removed the rubber hose and closed the window. Climbing out, I knocked the magazines to the floor. One slid forward and blocked the door. I shoved it back, and noticed the blurb for the lead article; *Is Fallout Threatening Your Future?* It was hardly the time for reading, but I picked up the magazine and glanced through it. The guy was on the old mutation pitch. If so and so many genes were irradiated by so and so many roentgens we would breed so and so many little monsters, one of which might be yours. I don't know why they always assume that a mutation necessarily has to be bad. As I recall my biology, mutations are why we're not still swinging from the trees by our tails with the other monkeys.

According to the writer, however, nuclear physicists were callous fellows gaily tossing radioactive poisons into the atmosphere without a thought to the possible effects on the human race. I had, of course, heard that theory expressed before; Nina herself had hurled similar accusations at me the day she came to the hospital to avenge Paul Hagen. It was fairly clear where she had got the notion; in fact Tony had blamed himself for shooting off his mouth around the house when he came to apologize later.

Standing there in the snow, I frowned at the magazine, tossed it in back, and picked up another. It wasn't on the cover, this time, but I found it in the table of contents: *The Growing Menace of Radioactivity.* The third had an article explaining just how many cities the size of New York could be wiped out by one of the latest X-bombs, as it was called: something too secret to describe, but terrible. The fourth contained a piece entitled: *The Atom—Pandora's Box?* The thesis, at a glance, seemed to be that splitting the atom had been a big mistake and we should glue the damn thing back together again quick like a bunny.

Anyone who has read the history of science will give a rueful little laugh when he comes across this sort of crap. There hasn't been a scientific advance yet that wasn't going to ruin the human race if we didn't quick stuff it back where it came from and forget all about it. When you have a little time, look up what they said about the steam engine, which was going to do all kinds of dreadful things to the people reckless enough to allow themselves to be snatched through space in a railroad car at the unthinkable speed of twenty miles per hour. . . .

When I came back to the Pontiac, Van was coming along the path with an armload of gear. I helped him load it into the trunk.

"You really travel equipped," he said. "We could have used some of this stuff last night."

"I hope you had a nice miserable time," I said.

"Still mad, eh?" he said.

"I haven't heard any apologies," I said.

He grinned. "If I went around apologizing to everybody whose feelings I had to hurt in the line of duty, I'd never have time for anything else. What's the dope on the kid in there? Did he try to kill himself or was it somebody else's idea?"

I shrugged. "He still hasn't said. But when we found him there was a fresh bump on his head; and a jeep had come out of the canyon shortly before we started in."

"How do you figure the motive?"

"My guess is that somebody doesn't like keeping failures on the payroll, particularly when they lose their nerve and take to the hills. Somebody was afraid the boy was scared enough to talk. Anyway, that was my hunch, which was why I thought we'd better come after him when we discovered he'd run away."

Van nodded slowly. He looked around at the rock and snow of the canyon. "I guess I'm just a city boy at heart," he said. "This kind of country scares hell out of me."

"It scares me, too," I said. "That's why I like it. What's the fun of tackling something easy?"

"For a respected scientist," he said, "you have some very juvenile attitudes. Well, let's get out of here before my feet freeze up again."

We brought the boy down last of all. The cold air set him coughing badly; I was glad the heater had been running long enough to warm up the interior of the car thoroughly. Nina got in back with him; Van and his stooge joined me in front, each with a shovel. I gunned the engine, backed up as far as she would go, and took a running start across the brief clear space where the car had been standing. It was the first time that I really appreciated those two hundred horsepower. We hit the deep stuff hard, swerved, straightened out, and kept on moving. It was downhill, which helped; and the weight of five passengers and the gear in the trunk also helped.

We made half a mile before a drift stopped us. I backed up and hit it twice more, but couldn't break through. The last time she wouldn't back out of it, either. The shovel brigade turned out; and I got out to open the hood and push the snow out of the radiator. They got it out from under the wheels and cleared something of a lane and got behind and pushed. We made twenty yards and stuck again. They shoveled some more. We made another twenty. They shoveled again. We pulled clear and kept on going, but they had to run after me a quarter of a mile before I found a place where I could stop with some hope of getting started again.

Then we had a long downhill run along an open hillside where the snow had blown thin, followed by a mean climb where it had drifted three feet deep and had to be shoveled all the way to the top. I spelled Van for a while when he showed signs of weakening. In the middle of the afternoon we passed the fire where I had found them, still smoking. Some time later we passed their car, half-buried in the snow. I was surprised they had got that far without chains. We had to dig it out and nudge it aside with the Pontiac before we could squeeze past on the narrow road.

It was five o'clock and twilight when we reached the end

of the canyon, having spent four hours covering six miles.
The state road had not been plowed, but a truck of some
kind had come through leaving tracks that were like a paved
highway after the stuff through which we had been driving.
We only had to dig out twice in the next nineteen miles. The
sky was clearing. The main highway had been plowed when
we got to it. We reached the hospital in Espanola a little
after seven, turned the boy over to the doctors, and sat
down to wait for them to tell us something.

Presently Van came in the hospital front door, looked
around, spotted us sitting there, and came over.

"How's it going?" he asked.

Nina shook her head. "Nobody's told us anything yet."

"Well, your brother's in good hands. Come on out and
I'll buy you both dinner."

"Thanks, but I'd rather wait here." She glanced at me.
"You go ahead, Jim. I'll be all right."

I put back the magazine I had been reading. "Well, I'll
bring you back a sandwich and some coffee."

Outside it was clear and cold. There was some snow
around, but not very much. You would not think fifty miles
and a thousand feet of altitude would make so much difference.

"That's a nice girl," Van said.

"How much are you selling her for?" I asked.

"What . . . Oh." He laughed.

I said, "If I should decide to divorce my present wife
and marry Miss Rasmussen, I'll remember that I have your
blessing."

He said, "Okay. You don't have to hit me with a brick;
I'll mind my own business."

Espanola is a small town on the upper Rio Grande, big
enough to have a movie and, as I recall, a traffic light, but
not much else. It's not as much of a tourist trap as most of
those places, since it's a little off the beaten track. The café
we entered specialized in Mexican food. It was late and I
was hungry enough to take a chance on my rebuilt digestive
tract; I ordered the standard mess of tacos, enchiladas, and
frijoles, which are beans. Van ordered a hamburger and coffee. It wasn't a comfortable meal; we didn't have much to
say to each other.

When I returned to the hospital, Nina was not in the
waiting room. A nurse said she was with her brother. I sat
down and read a magazine. It was getting late and there

wasn't anybody in the place except an expectant father who seemed to be taking it pretty hard considering that, from what he said to the nurse, he was waiting for his fifth. Well, I was hardly in a position to sit in judgment on him, not having been through it even once, myself. The print became hard to keep in focus. When I opened my eyes, Nina was standing over me. She did not speak at once.

I sat up and said, "I brought your sandwich. I'm afraid the coffee's cold by now. How is he?"

"They've got him full of sulfapyridine," she said. "They say he has . . . a good chance."

I looked up at her. She was so tired she was swaying. "Sit down and eat something," I said, unwrapping the sandwich for her. "Then we'll find you a place to sleep."

She sat down beside me. "It's all right," she said. "One of the nurses is a darling; she's fixed me up in a room they're not using. Jim?"

"Yes?"

"Does 'Ararat' mean anything to you?"

"Not except as a mountain in the Bible. Why?"

"After you left the cabin to get help this morning, he woke up. We talked a little. He wasn't very coherent, but he knew me. I mean, he wasn't delirious. I asked him . . . what I thought you'd want to know. About your wife. He said 'Ararat Number Three.' "

"Ararat Number Three. Did he say anything else?"

"He said 'mine.' Then he said 'uranium' and laughed. When he laughed, it hurt him, and he stopped talking. Later he started to cough. I didn't get to ask anything else. I'm sorry."

I said, "You did fine. I'm very grateful."

"It's not much. I hope it helps you find her."

We looked at each other for a moment. I said, "Yes, I guess that comes first, doesn't it?" I got to my feet; and she rose also.

She said, "It's funny. I used to hate you." After a silence she said, "It was just a kiss. It doesn't obligate you in any way. Remember that."

"Sure," I said. "Well, so long, Spanish."

"Jim." She looked down, unfastened the two lower buttons of her wool shirt, and reached inside. "Here," she said. "You may need this, wherever you're going. You can't always carry that big rifle with you."

I looked down at the pistol she was offering me: a .22 automatic with a slim, short barrel. The weapon was familiar.

I had had an opportunity to study it carefully from the wrong end some months before. The police must have given it back to her. I looked from the gun to her face. She blushed. It was an interesting phenomenon, and one you don't see very often these days.

"I—" she said, and stopped.

"I'm hurt, Spanish," I said. "You didn't trust me. You brought a gun along to protect yourself from me."

"Yes," she said, "and there was a time or two when it looked as if I might need it, too." Her smile faded and she looked at me steadily. "Bring it back if you can," she said. "If not, it doesn't matter. Don't worry about it. Good luck."

EIGHTEEN

A HUNDRED YEARS ago, if you'd been snowbound up in the Chama country, it would have taken you a decent number of days to work your way back to civilization as represented by Santa Fe, and even then the transition would not have been overwhelming, since Sante Fe was a fairly crude town at the time. Today you can practically step out of a snowdrift into a hot shower. It puts a strain on a man's adaptability. What it did to me was upset my digestion, or perhaps I should put the blame on the enchiladas.

I had a rough night; in the morning, the worst was over, but I felt weak and tired. Also I seemed to be catching cold again. It seemed advisable to take things easy lest I wind up back on the sick list; I had tea and toast sent up to the room, and called the hospital in Espanola and was told Miss Rasmussen was sleeping and her brother was holding his own. I got a boy to run the Pontiac to a garage with orders to tighten any nuts and bolts that might have worked loose, wash and grease the thing, and hang onto it until I came or called. Then I hung out a *Do Not Disturb* sign and slept until two o'clock in the afternoon. I had some clear bouillon sent up although I was hungry enough for steak.

I started to call Espanola again, but stopped when I realized that I was much less interested in how her brother was making out than in just talking to her; and we didn't really have a great deal to talk about. I hung up the phone, therefore, found a pencil and paper and, sitting in bed, wrote:

Ararat #3
Mine
Uranium (*laughter*)

It looked like a neat puzzle for Sherlock Holmes. I got on the phone again and called a lawyer I had met socially. He said that a lot of mines had screwy names like that— Biblical names, in particular, were quite commonplace—but

119

that tracking down the location of the property was a little out of his line. He referred me to a man named Garcia who, since I could not come to the office, sent over a young fellow named Montoya—the Garcias and Montoyas are the Smiths and Joneses of New Mexico. Bob Montoya turned out to be a nice-looking dark kid in his early twenties. They run to extremes. A nice-looking Spanish-American kid you would trust with your life and your daughter's virtue; a mean-looking one looks as if he'd slit your throat for a nickel and give back four cents' change.

"I get the idea, Dr. Gregory," Montoya said after I'd explained the situation as far as I thought necessary, which wasn't very far. "I'll see what I can do for you, but I'd better warn you it could turn out to be a tough and expensive assignment. Nobody knows just how many people are wandering around out there with Geiger counters staking claims they figure will make them rich by Christmas; and their notions of surveying are pretty inaccurate. There's supposed to be at least one county up in Utah where the filed claims add up to twice the total area of the county. . . . It looks to me as if what you've got here is the name of the hole and not the company, if you get what I mean. I'd say a couple of fellows calling themselves, say, the Jackrabbit Mining Association, had at least three claims which they called Ararat One, Two, and Three. That's the usual custom. Do you know anything about uranium mining, Dr. Gregory?"

I really didn't know a great deal about how the stuff got out of the ground and into the laboratory. I said, "Not very much. I hope to learn."

He grinned, his teeth very white in his dark face. *"Sí, Señor.* So hope about a million other people. I suppose you've got a kind of roundabout tip on this Ararat property?" I nodded. He said, "You can't tell me any more about it?"

"No," I said. "That's all I've got to go on."

"Well, I'll do my best to find it for you." He rose from his chair and grinned at me wisely. "I suppose you want it kept real quiet."

If I'd told him I wanted just the opposite, it would only have confused him. "Well, don't broadcast it," I said, and watched him go out, and hoped he would not run into trouble but could see no reason why he should, since I had made sure his boss and the lawyer also knew I was looking for a mine called Ararat. It seemed unlikely that anyone would tackle the job of silencing us all.

The following morning I woke up strong and healthy. I called Espanola and learned that, barring complications, the patient would live. Miss Rasmussen was not in the building, which was just as well. I had the garage send my car around, checked out of the hotel, and drove down to Albuquerque. It was a clear and beautiful spring day, so warm that I had the windows open. If it had snowed down here at all, no traces remained. The Sandia Mountains made a friendly and home-like shape behind town as I approached; the air was so clear that I could see the TV towers on the crest quite distinctly, even at this distance. I picked up some groceries at the near-by shopping center, drove home and parked in the drive, and carried the stuff inside. The house was cold and empty. It seemed much too big for one person. I made myself some lunch in the kitchen, feeling like a tramp camping out in a barn.

Eating, I read the mail that had been stuffed into the box while I was away. One envelope had no stamp; it had apparently been delivered by hand. I knew an odd little mo-ment of expectancy as I tore it open, but the slip of paper inside bore the heading: *William Walsh Enterprises, Inc.* The typewritten note asked Dr. James Gregory to call Mr. William Walsh at the Alvarado Hotel at his earliest convenience. I leaned back, snared the kitchen phone, and got the number. A switchboard operator and a secretary later, I had my father-in-law on the line.

"Hi, Pop," I said. "When did you get into town?"

"Where the hell have you been?" he demanded. "I've been trying to reach you for two days. Where can we talk? I'm tied up this afternoon; but how about the bar downstairs at five o'clock?"

"Five's fine," I said. "Be seeing you, Pop."

The kitchen clock read a little after twelve. I got up and washed the dishes and put things away. I went out and organized the gear in the trunk of the car, but did not un-pack. Instead, I replaced the supplies we had consumed up in the mountains. I took the .270 into the house, cleaned and oiled it thoroughly since it had been wet, and put it back into the trunk. That made the car ready. All it needed was a place to go.

I went back into the house. It seemed as empty as a vacuum chamber. I opened Natalie's door. The black-and-white room had a well-preserved and lifeless look, like a bedroom at Mount Vernon. I closed the door and went into my own room, drew the Venetian blind, sat down on the bed, took out Nina Rasmussen's little .22 automatic and cleaned it. The clip was fully loaded. It held ten cartridges. She had not given the gun to me with a shell in the chamber and I did not jack one in now; I'd rather risk being a little slow getting a shot off when I wanted it than have one go off when I didn't want it. I tucked the weapon back inside my shirt. Wearing it was both illegal and uncomfortable, but I didn't want to leave it around where anyone could see it. A .22 isn't much of a firearm, but a .22 that nobody knew I had might come in handy. At four-thirty I dressed and drove downtown.

The bar of the Alvarado Hotel is an insult to New Mexico, being a dead ringer for any New York cocktail lounge. What's the point of living in the great southwest if you have to do your drinking in a chrome-plated martini trap to the tune of, so help me, a character with a Hawaiian guitar? Not that I've got a thing against martinis, or Hawaiians, either; but I do like a little local atmosphere with my drinks. Mr. Walsh was sitting in a booth dictating to an earnest young lady with a notebook and horn-rimmed glasses. He waved her away when he saw me coming. Receding, she looked less earnest and more interesting; I found myself wondering if her duties involved anything besides typing and shorthand, which was probably unfair to my father-in-law. He was a solid, medium-sized man with stiff gray hair cut quite short all over his head. The steel-gray hair made a nice contrast to the deep sun-tan he had picked up somewhere recently, probably in Florida. I don't know anything about men like William Walsh, and I make no effort to learn. His daughter is a big enough problem for me to try to solve. I had wired him the bare details the night she disappeared, and had not been in communication with him since.

Mr. Walsh said, "Sit down, boy. Where the hell have you been hiding? I've been trying to get in touch with you ever since I got your wire."

"So you said over the phone," I said, sitting down facing him.

"What'll it be?"

"A martini, I guess." As I said, I've nothing against them; I just prefer to drink them, out here, in tequila-and-pulque surroundings.

Mr. Walsh caught the eye of the waitress and she came right over, which indicated that he must have done some heavy tipping during his short stay. Usually they're almost as hard to catch as desert antelope.

"Another of the same for me," he said, pushing a tall glass in her direction. "And a martini for my son-in-law; and none of that tired old bar mix, sister. Have him make it up fresh: Noilly Prat vermouth and Gordon's gin, one to five —is that about right, Greg?"

"One to five is fine," I said.

"Yeah," he said. "And none of those damn olives, sister. Just a twist of lemon. Got it?"

Now, I like the olive in a martini; you can't eat a lemon peel. But I wouldn't have spoiled his act for the world. I looked around the place. It was scantily filled with the usual bunches of men. In Albuquerque they have an odd custom: they leave the women home and the men go out to dinner together. I suppose there's nothing actually wrong with this, but it looks queer to the transplanted easterner, besides making the scenery very dull: who wants to look at tables full of men?

"Well," Mr. Walsh said, "they haven't found her yet, they tell me."

"No," I said.

"They seem to think she may be mixed up in a murder. Not to mention a lot of other things."

"So I've been told," I said.

"Do you believe it?"

I looked at him. "I don't believe anything, or disbelieve it, either. It's not my job to prove my wife guilty; and I'll wait to prove her innocent until I've heard some specific charges. Right now all I want is to find her."

"Are you working on it? Is that where you've been?"

I nodded. "And I have a clue, for what it's worth," I said, and told him about it.

"Ararat Number Three," he said thoughtfully. "Hell, you should have got in touch with me yesterday, instead of ringing in this yokel up in Santa Fe. I've got the boys who can track it down and never let anybody know they're looking. You'd better get on the phone and call him off; this has got to be handled right—"

"No," I said.

"What do you mean?"

"It's got to be handled wrong," I said. "As wrong and as obviously as it can be done without looking phony. I *want* these people to know I'm on their track. They'll find out by watching young Montoya."

"It looks to me," he said, "as if you were asking for trouble, boy."

I said, "Any trouble I get on top of what I've already got, I wouldn't even notice, Pop." I never could call him "Dad" because that's what I had called my own father while he was alive; and "Mr. Walsh" sounded too formal. Besides, I guess I always felt the need to show I wasn't really impressed by all that money.

He studied me across the table. "Has it occurred to you—" He paused and drank from his glass. "Has it occurred to you that the kid may have good reason for not wanting to be found? She always did have a lot of screwball ideas. Not that I think she—" He let the sentence die. I did not say anything. He took another swallow. "What's the matter with kids these days, anyway? They get themselves in the damnedest jams!"

I watched him for a while longer, until he looked away. I got up. "Thanks for the drink, Pop," I said. "I'll be seeing you."

When I pulled up in the drive, the house was dark. There was no reason it shouldn't be, of course, since I had left no light on. I started along the concrete walk toward the front door, and something broke out of the ornamental shrubbery by the garage and came for me. There was no time to dig through topcoat, suitcoat, and shirt for the gun; I simply threw myself down and back, into it, hitting it low, bringing it down as neatly as if I'd played football for dear old Chicago, which hasn't got a team.

Then I rolled over and came to my hands and knees facing Ruth DeVry who was sitting on the lawn with one shoe off and her hair in her face, gasping for the breath I had knocked out of her.

NINETEEN

I GOT UP and brushed myself off—painfully, since I had taken a heavy blow across the back. Ruth did not move except to hug herself, gasping. There were no knives or pistols on the grass around her, and her hands were empty. I went over and picked her up by the armpits and set her on her feet. For all her narrow look, she was no feather. I found her missing shoe, one of those ballet-slipper things, and held it so she could put her foot in it.

"Don't jump out behind me like that, Ruth," I said. "My reflexes aren't under very good control these days. Come on in the house."

Inside, I closed the door behind us and turned on the hall light. She stopped at the mirror to pat her hair into place; then pulled her glasses off and set them back straight. Tonight they had big white rims set with some kind of sparkling stones. She always said that she wasn't ashamed of having to wear them and wasn't going to have anybody thinking she was, either. Besides the jeweled glasses, she was wearing a pair of those tight kneepants women have been inserting themselves into of late, that are undoubtedly the most unbecoming garments to be invented since the beach pajamas I barely remember as a kid. These were of black velveteen or some similar material. She was also wearing a loose and rather flimsy short-sleeved sweater, white with shiny gold threads, and some copper bracelets that clashed when she moved her arms. The whole outfit looked like a kind of arty cocktail costume that had not quite jelled. Being thrown for a ten-yard loss accounted for part of her disorganized appearance, but not all; I remembered that she was always having these bright ideas about clothes that didn't quite pan out.

She spoke at last. "I was driving by this afternoon and saw your car outside so I knew you were back. . . . I've been waiting *hours* for you to get home! Freezing slowly to death! And then you knock me down and walk all over me!"

She laughed ruefully, and turned to face me. "What got into you anyway, Greg?"

I said, "I'm sorry. The last person who came at me like that had a knife."

"A knife! Heavens, you really lead an exciting life these days!"

"Uh-huh," I said. "What with friends hiding in the bushes and popping out at me like champagne corks."

She laughed again. "I was just . . . just going to fall on your neck and sob out my tale of woe. You certainly spoiled my big moment but good, darling." She drew a long breath. "Well, are you going to ask me into the living room and offer me a drink?"

"Sure."

I let her go by me, and followed her in, switching on lights as I came to them. She turned to face me in the middle of the room.

"It isn't really funny, Greg. It isn't funny at all. Look."

She touched the tip of a finger to her lip and held the finger out for me to examine. I couldn't see anything on it.

She said, a little annoyed: "Well, it was bleeding earlier! Look here!"

She leaned forward, pulling at her lip to show me. It might have been slightly swollen, and there might even have been a small cut, but you know how inconspicuous those lip-cuts are, once they stop bleeding. They feel big, but you can't see them.

"Did I do that?" I asked.

"No, he did."

"Who?"

"Larry, of course!"

The thought of little Larry DeVry hauling off and socking his wife in the teeth didn't make good sense; and if it had happened I wanted no part of their family row.

I said, "Well, he's probably sorry by now. Why don't you run along home—"

"Sorry!" she cried. "You don't know what he's like these days! He's always been a surly and impossible person to live with—you've no idea of all the things I've put up with all these years, darling—but lately he's turned positively ugly. I mean, I'm truly afraid of him, Greg. I really am. He's not . . . I think he's actually a little crazy. He imagines things!"

"Such as?"

"Just . . . just things. About me. Insane things—" Her

face kind of crumpled and tears started running down it. She sank down on the near-by sofa and sat there, crying helplessly. You have to be very much in love with a girl to like her when she cries. I discovered that any tender feelings I might once have had—or imagined I had—for Ruth DeVry, were long since gone.

"I'll get you that drink," I said.

"No, don't go. Please! Just sit down and . . . and be nice to me, Greg. I've had such an awful time. I'm so m-miserable I just want to die."

I stood there awkwardly. I had no intention of sitting down beside her, knowing perfectly well that the minute I did she would fling her arms about me and weep on my coat; and it was perfectly possible that, since we were old friends, and since I was somewhat less innocent and idealistic these days than I had been in Chicago, one thing might lead to another, even without any tender feelings being involved. . . . It was not a matter of being faithful to my wife, who had after all left me to go to Reno, nor was it a matter of being faithful to anybody else, or even of being loyal to my old, if somewhat tarnished, friendship with this woman's husband. It was simply a matter of my life being complicated enough already without complicating it further with Ruth DeVry.

I was saved from embarrassment by a knock at the door. Ruth came to her feet abruptly. "It's Larry!" she gasped. "If he finds me here—"

I said, "Sit down and relax, Ruth." I went to the door and pulled it open. It was Larry, all right. "Come in and join the party," I said.

"Is Ruth here?"

"Yes," I said. "I don't know why, but she's here."

His face had a funny, intent look. "She mentioned seeing your car this afternoon. I thought I might find her here. Now that Jack Bates is no longer with us."

I said, "With a little effort, that could be developed into a dirty story. Come in and work on it while I get us all something to drink."

He hesitated, watching me through his heavy glasses. There's always something a little sinister about a man with thick-lensed spectacles, perhaps because they're standard equipment for every mad scientist in the movies.

"I'll come in," Larry said at last. "But I won't drink your liquor, Greg."

"Suit yourself," I said, and let him pass me, and closed the door without turning my back to him. Everybody seemed to be acting a little cracked tonight, and there was no sense in taking unnecessary chances. Entering the living room behind him, I looked at Ruth, who had settled back on the sofa. Except that she had all her clothes on, she looked pretty much like what a jealous husband might expect to find: her face was flushed, and her hair still a little mussed from our recent collision. There was dust on her velveteen pants; and the thin, glinting sweater had slid down to show part of her shoulder. She looked rumpled and rather attractive; some women look their best with a high polish, but others do better with part of it knocked off. "Larry's not drinking with us," I said. "A matter of principle, I understand. What'll it be, Ruth?"

She shook her head, watching her husband with a wary and yet defiant attitude.

Larry said, "Well, here are are. It's very cosy, isn't it? I suppose it was inevitable. Three years of pretending to be deaf and blind are enough, Greg."

I said, "That remark was too subtle for me. You'd better develop it further."

He said, "I'm just a stupid little mathematician, to quote my wife. It takes me quite a while to learn what goes on behind my back. I suppose it started back in Chicago when you used to stay at the apartment. You handled that very neatly, I must say, both of you. I never suspected a thing."

"There was nothing to suspect."

"No? You must take me for a complete fool, Greg! Did you think I could go forever without figuring out why you asked me to join the Project? Particularly when you made it so obvious that it wasn't my ideas you wanted; all you really needed was a hack mathematician to make routine calculations, and that was all you ever intended for me to be here. . . . But it was a mistake to ask Jack Bates here, wasn't it? He was younger and better looking; he took her away from you, didn't he? For a while, at least. Until he died."

I looked at him for a while. At a moment like that you wonder if the guy has always been this way and you just never saw it; or whether he changed when you weren't looking. Maybe, I reflected, I should get into the habit of taking a good hard look at the people around me, every now and then, just to check up.

I said, "That's a very interesting thesis, Larry. It seems strange, under the circumstances, that I bothered to get married, doesn't it?"

He laughed sharply. "Not strange at all. A rich wife is an asset to a penniless scientist, if he isn't burdened with too many scruples. Besides making good camouflage for an illicit love affair. . . . You must have handled Natalie badly, though; she saw through the situation and left you fast enough!"

I said, "I'm really a hell of a fellow, aren't I? A sonofabitch like I am would be apt to get a big kick out of knocking another fellow's teeth in, wouldn't he?"

"I might have expected that reaction," he said stiffly. "You always did have a muscular mentality, Greg. It was always a surprise to me that you ever managed to show signs of a genuine scientific imagination—or did you? A man who would steal other men's wives wouldn't be above stealing their ideas, would he?" He walked quickly to the hall door. "Never mind threatening me again, I'm going. I'll leave the two of you alone." He laughed harshly. "But before you relax in Ruth's gentle company, just ask yourself one question, Greg. Ask yourself how the scarf that fell out of the pocket of Natalie's fur coat when Ruth was hanging it up in the closet that night—you remember the scarf, don't you?—well, just ask yourself how it got from our house to the vicinity of Jack Bates's dead body!"

His footsteps marched down the hall. The door closed loudly. The steps went down the walk outside. A car started and drove away. Ruth was on her feet, reaching for me. There are some women who can't ask you the time unless they've got a good grip on you. I side-stepped.

"You see how he is!" she gasped. "You see how suspicious and unreasonable—"

"I see," I said. "I see that you've teased the poor guy crazy with things that never happened—and maybe a few that did."

Her face became hard and ugly. She, too, was someone I had never known. "Oh, so it's my fault!"

"Not entirely," I said. "I'll admit that a man's got to cooperate in order for anybody to make that big a fool of him."

She threw back her head and laughed shrilly. "Look who's talking about fools!" she cried. "Just look who's calling another man a fool!"

"Good night, Ruth," I said.

"Well, if that's the way you feel—" She walked quickly to the door, paused to pull her sweater straight, and turned quickly to look at me again. None of them can just walk out of the house. She said, "As for the scarf—"

I said, "To hell with the damn scarf."

She glared at me for a moment, whirled, and ran out, slamming the front door. I needed a drink. I went into the kitchen and pulled open the refrigerator. It was sitting right there on the shelf, propped up against a milk carton—as far as I know you can't buy milk in glass in New Mexico, it's all in cardboard. It was a cheap envelope without address or other writing. It seemed like an odd place to use as a mailbox; yet very logical when you came to think of it. The refrigerator was the last place anyone else would search for a hidden communication, yet it was a place I would be bound to look sooner or later, at the very latest for my breakfast eggs.

I took it out by the edges and pushed the door closed with fingertip. It seemed unlikely that fingerprints would mean anything, but somebody might get upset if I neglected the more obvious precautions. I slit the envelope with the small, sharp blade of my knife—the same knife I had used against Tony Rasmussen, but not the same blade. Everything was different these days: refrigerators were mailboxes and penknives were lethal weapons and old friends turned into snarling and suspicious beasts. I blew into the slit, and drew out the folded sheet of paper inside, unfolded it carefully, and read the message printed in block letters with a soft pencil:

BRING FIFTY THOUSAND IN USED BILLS TO HANKSVILLE UTAH IF YOU WANT HER BACK ALIVE.

TWENTY

EARLY IN MY brief western career I bought myself a pair of cowboy boots. That was the year I did all the bear hunting up around Chama, on horseback; and the old fellow who took me out recommended this type of footgear highly for riding. He was quite right. The boots were fine for riding—but I never learned to walk in them. You've got to start young to get used to those heels, Nevertheless. I broke them out now, since they had certain advantages none of my other boots possessed. They pulled on instead of lacing, for one thing; a definite asset to a man stiffened by an assortment of scars and lacerations. They gave me a couple of inches more height, also; there's nothing like a cowboy boot to make you feel tall and reckless and daring, and I could use that feeling. The open tops were handy for a purpose I had in mind; and I didn't think I was going to have to walk very far, anyway. I was just pulling them on, having dressed in my hunting clothes complete to the long johns, when the doorbell rang.

I swaggered across the living room in my jeans and high heels, and opened up. It was the girl with the horn-rimmed glasses who had been taking dictation from Mr. Walsh in the bar of the Alvarado. She was wearing a light spring coat and a small hat with a rudimentary veil, and she was carrying a rectangular package.

"Please step back into the light," she said. "I can't see your face clearly." I took a step backwards. She nodded. "All right, Dr. Gregory. Here it is. Mr. Walsh says good luck." She smiled and put the package into my hand. She was really a very pretty girl, despite the glasses. "So do I," she said. "Good night."

I watched her get into a light sedan that had the anonymous look of a rental car, and drive away. I closed the door. It was the first time I had ever had fifty thousand dollars in my possession at one time, but it did not make my heart beat any faster. I can get excited over a deer, or a scientific discovery, or a mathematical equation, or even a pretty girl, but where money is concerned I have nerves of steel. Five minutes later I was in the car, driving north.

They let me get almost to Bernalillo, which is a small town eighteen miles north of Albuquerque. Then a state police cruiser pulled away from a filling station as I passed, passed me, and cut in ahead of me, hitting the siren lightly. This was not altogether unexpected, and I followed it out on the shoulder and came to a stop behind it. A blue-clad officer got out and came walking back to me.

"Dr. Gregory?" he said. "Dr. James Gregory?"

"Yes," I said.

"May I see your driving license, please?"

I held it out. He examined it and passed it back. I asked, "What's the trouble, officer?"

"I couldn't say, sir. We'll just wait here a few minutes. They'll be along pretty soon."

He had a dark, grave face. It wasn't worth while trying to argue with him. It's never worth while arguing with a policeman; and it's particularly useless when he is not of your own race and religion, because the difference is always there, cutting both ways, even if you are both intelligent and tolerant men.

I said, "Sit in the car where it's warm, if you like."

He shook his head, thanking me politely. Maybe there was a rule against it. We waited ten to fifteen minutes. Cars and trucks passed; and people looked out of them with the sympathetic but rather wary interest aroused by the sight of a fellow-citizen in trouble with the law. Finally we heard the sound of a car approaching from the south at considerably more than the legal rate of speed, which, in New Mexico on the open road is sixty miles per hour in the daytime and fifty-five at night. The policeman looked up with professional interest. I wondered how close he could clock them by ear. The car slowed down and came to a squealing and crunching halt behind us. The policeman walked back to meet it. Presently he came past me again, and got into the cruiser, which drove away. There was a tap on the glass of the right-hand door of the Pontiac. I leaned over to release the lock. Van Horn pulled the door open. There was a man behind him.

I said, "Leave the stooge outside."

The man didn't like that. I didn't like him. I was no longer much taken with Van Horn either. This passion for little men with badges that has swept the country recently is something I find hard to understand. I was brought up on the theory that a cop was a necessary evil and you tried to get along with as few of him as possible.

Van Horn said, "All right, Johnson, wait in the car," and Johnson went back along the gravel, unhappily. Van Horn got in beside me and closed the door. "How's the Rasmussen boy getting along?" he asked casually.

"All right, the last I heard," I said.

He glanced at me, and at the departing agent. "Why antagonize people, Greg?"

"Are cops people?" I asked. "I thought they were just like game wardens."

He said, "You talk big, but I bet you haven't shot over your bag limit in fifteen years."

"The amount of game left in this country, a man is practically forced to be a sportsman in self-defense," I said. "When I was a kid, however, the warden and I didn't get along at all well. That was part of the fun. Nowadays when you see a badge you get down on hands and knees and touch your forehead to the ground respectfully. Particularly if it's a federal badge. Have you got a federal badge, Van?"

"I could probably borrow one if I needed it."

"I noticed the state police do what you tell them." After a moment I said, "Don't tell them again, Van. Next time I won't stop."

He said, "Don't get tough with me, Greg."

"I'm not getting tough with you. I'm just telling you. Next time I'll keep going. They'll have to shoot to stop me."

"We'll talk about that in a minute," he said. "First let me see the letter."

I took it out of the pocket of my wool shirt and gave it to him, and switched on the dome light for him. "I won't be naïve and ask how you knew about that," I said. "I figured my telephone was probably tapped by this time. Us subversives can't expect much privacy. Well, I hope you enjoyed eavesdropping on my conversation with my father-in-law."

"Hanksville, Utah," he said. "Anybody can write a note."

I reached into my pocket. "Sure. And anybody can enclose with it a gold wedding ring engraved: James-Natalie 1951. From Vladivostok. Or Outer Mongolia. Or Novosibirsk. Or Moscow. Nuts." I looked at the ring, small and shiny on my palm. He held out his hand. I let the ring slide from my hand to his. "You don't have to run tests on it," I said. "It's hers."

He looked at it and gave it back. "Perhaps we owe Mrs. Gregory an apology," he said.

"Yes," I said. "But you don't really believe that. The ring doesn't prove anything. She could have taken it off before she left the country, as you think she was trying to do. Or they could have killed her and got it off the body. A week is a long time for kidnapers to wait before sending a ransom note—you'd know more about that than I do. Or she could be working with them, luring me to my doom. Does that cover all possibilities?"

"Not quite," he said. "She could have thrown it in your face as she left for Reno. It's one way for a woman to dispose of an unwanted wedding ring. And you could have decided to put on a little act for me to clear her reputation—and incidentally your own. As the husband of a kidnap victim you'd look a lot better to certain people in Washington and the Project than as the husband of a mysterious disappearance. A refrigerator is an odd place to leave a ransom note—you did tell Mr. Walsh you found it in the refrigerator, didn't you? I can't recall anybody ever using that drop before."

I said, "Van, you're cute." I looked at the ring, took out my wallet and placed the ring carefully in a safe compartment and returned the wallet to my pocket.

He asked, "Why didn't you notify the police?"

I said, "Maybe I figured I didn't need to, with a bug on my telephone. You're here, aren't you?"

He shook his head. "That won't do, Greg."

"No?" I said. "Well, let's put it this way, then. I didn't notify the police or the F.B.I. because they would undoubtedly have tried to stop me just as you doubtless intend to. They are not primarily interested in Natalie's safety and neither are you. I am. And I don't intend to be stopped, Van. This may even be a straightforward deal; I can't take the chance that it isn't. And even if it isn't, I have certain theories about the people with whom we're dealing. I may be walking into a trap, but I don't have a great deal of respect for their traps. You get a feeling about people just like you get about game; there are the tough hunts and the easy ones. These people don't strike me as tough. I wouldn't dream of stacking myself against a real underworld kidnap gang, but I'm willing to take a chance against this outfit. I think I can bust out of any trap they set for me; yes, and take Natalie right out with me. Anyway, I'm going to try."

He shook his head. "Maybe you're willing, but it's a chance we can't afford to take. I'm sorry, Greg," he said. "We can't let you go. I'll have to ask you to come back to town with me."

"Uh-huh."

"Normally," he said, "the Bureau would probably advise payment. As a matter of fact, if Mr. Walsh wants to go to Hanksville with the money, I'll see that he gets all the co-operation he needs."

I said, "If he goes, nobody'll give him a tumble. If they'd wanted Bill Walsh, they'd have left a note for Bill Walsh."

"You see that, do you?"

I said, "I make a few deductions, too, in my line of work."

"It smells like a trap to me," he said.

"Sure."

"A kidnaping for money just doesn't fit in with anything else that's happened. I think they're after you. They've tried to kill you twice—three times, if you count the Rasmussen girl's attempt, which may or may not have been an independent venture—" He waited as if expecting me to comment; but I saw no point in getting into an argument over Nina. He said, "I wouldn't be surprised if they considered you dangerous game by this time. They might even be having trouble finding men willing to tackle the job, after what happened to Hagen and young Rasmussen. At least not without much more elaborate preparations than before. Do you know Hanksville?"

"I've heard of it and looked it up on the map. I've driven through that general part of Utah."

"Well, then you know more about it than I do. But I know from magazine articles that it's in the most desolate part of the uranium country, a hundred miles from nowhere—"

"To be exact," I said, "sixty miles from Green River, which isn't exactly a metropolis to start with." I looked at him. "Cut out the horsing around, Van. I've told you what I'm going to do and why. Tell me how you're going to stop me."

He said, "Be reasonable, Greg. Realize my position. Let's say that I have complete faith in your loyalty—"

"You have a damn funny way of showing it."

He went on without pausing: "Let's say, even, that I fully believe your wife to be an unwilling prisoner of a gang of kidnapers. Under ordinary conditions, any risks you might want to run for her would be your own business. But the conditions aren't ordinary. The government has a considerable investment in you, Greg; and it's my duty to protect that investment."

I said, "That's very neat. The government doesn't trust me to work for it, won't pay me a salary, but still claims the right to tell me to sit and twiddle my thumbs while my wife is in danger. If I let her be killed, does that make me trustworthy enough to go back to work at the Project?"

"Look," he said, "I understand your feelings perfectly—"

I said, "I don't think you do, Van. Reach back and pull that blanket off the rear seat." He did so. I asked, "What do you see?"

"A rifle and a double-barreled shotgun," he said.

"They're both loaded," I said. "I wasn't kidding, Van. Don't send any more cops to stop me. They're nice hard-working guys and we'd hate to lose any of them. I'm a dangerous man, pal. I've got high-heeled boots and a big hat. I've got two tons of car and an assortment of high-powered firearms. And I'm going to Hanksville, Utah."

He said, "You're bluffing."

"Try me and see."

"I don't think you're that crazy."

"I'm pretty damn crazy," I said. "I've been shot, knifed, more or less widowed, and suspended from my job. I've been called plain and fancy names and heard my wife called the same. By using a few brains, of which I seem to have a monopoly around here, I've got myself a tip on what's going on. Not much of a tip, but enough that when I started to follow it up, I got a reaction. Some people don't like the direction in which I'm working. I've forced a move out of them, which is more than anybody else has done—everybody else being too damn busy watching the posts and borders for hypothetical Russian spies. So now all of a sudden I'm too valuable to risk. Well, nuts to you, my fine federal friend. You have a couple of seconds in which to decide how badly you want to keep me here. The way to do it is pull out the gun you're undoubtedly packing and squeeze the trigger carefully. You get one shot free. We charge for the rest."

He sat beside me in silence for a space of time, while two cars whipped past from the south with a flash of head-lights, and a big semi-trailer job thundered past from the north. At last he laughed shortly.

"I still think you're bluffing," he said.

"Sure."

"I could have you arrested."

"You could try. Washington would love the publicity."

"I don't know why I gave up a nice peaceful job running down simple-minded criminals in order to come out here and ride herd on a bunch of temperamental intellectual screwballs."

I said, "Are we through showing each other how tough we are?"

"I wasn't—"

"The hell you weren't. Throwing cops at my head and ordering me back to town and threatening me with arrest. Can we talk like sensible people for a moment?"

"It would be a pleasant change," he said.

"Okay," I said. "I'm going to Hanksville. Short of shooting me, you can't stop me. I'm going in from the north by way of Green River since I don't know if I can make the road over Hite's Ferry in this Detroit dreamboat so early in the season. It's supposed to be a lulu. As you'll gather, I'm driving. That'll give you time to fly a man up to Moab or Green River and have him drift casually into Hanksville before I get there. Don't send anybody you're awfully fond of, because they'll undoubtedly be looking for him; they'll probably spot him since it's not much of a town, and they may be figuring to take him out fast when the action starts."

"I'll go myself," he said.

"That's fine," I said. "If you sent a nice guy and he got killed, somebody might miss him. And don't expect any help from me. I won't be dropping rose petals along the trail for you to follow. In fact, you can count on not getting a damn bit of co-operation from me. I'm going to play along with these birds, just as convincingly as I can, until I see what it's all about."

"And after that?"

"After that," I said, "we'll see how it breaks."

"I still think you're making a mistake," he said.

"Well, I'm sure you'll do your damnedest to save me from it," I said. "Just so you keep out of sight and don't spook the game, that's all I ask."

TWENTY-ONE

I HIT MOAB, UTAH, around ten in the morning, having crossed about a quarter of New Mexico and a small corner of Colorado during the night. You can make a lot better time on those straight southwestern highways, even the smaller ones, than you can back east on anything but a turnpike. Moab, the self-styled uranium capital of the world, was a small, feverish, boom-town sort of place even this early in the spring; every other vehicle on the street seemed to be a jeep and every other man a prospector. Every kind of equipment was being offered for sale or rent, from a geologist's pick to an airplane complete with pilot and scintillometer—I understand they do a lot of prospecting from the air these days. I had no interest in the town except gasoline; when the tank was full I climbed back in the car and kept on going, wishing Tony Rasmussen had seen fit to slice me in front instead of in back. I was rubbing pretty raw against the cushions from all the driving.

I reached Green River, a small desert town, early in the afternoon, and parked in front of a café that advertised a couple of popular brands of beer. These signs should not be taken too literally. Utah beer has only three per cent of what it takes, since the Mormons who run the state are abstemious people. Inside, the café had the lunch-counter look of a place where no serious drinking is done. There was a sign on the wall: *Why don't you spit on the ceiling? Any fool can spit on the floor!* Another read: *If you're so smart why ain't you rich?* A third declared: *No deals under $100,000 discussed at this bar.* There were two or three tables besides the counter and stools. I had a bottle of the emasculated beer while I waited for my food. Drinking it slowly, I looked around at the other customers. There weren't many, and none of them seemed interested in me.

After eating, I filled up the tank again, since I didn't know how long it might be before I got another chance. The man at the filling station said that if the weather stayed

138

dry I could probably get to Hanksville somehow if I was fool enough to try, but damned if he, personally, would take a good car over that road. I drove to the intersection four miles out of town and got the general drift of what he was talking about.

It was a dirt road leading to the south and west. At this point in Utah, according to my road map, there was nothing between me and Highway 66 crossing Arizona three hundred miles to the south except a lot of sand and rock, the Colorado River, and some Navajo Indians—that is, except for the road I was looking at and the town of Hanksville. If you dropped a couple of New England states into this blank space on the map you'd have a hard time finding them again. The road itself was dry, but that was all that could be said for it. It had obviously been very wet quite recently, perhaps during the same storm we had felt in New Mexico. Trucks had churned up the resulting mud and cut it into ruts; cars had stuck in it and been dug out by guys who weren't particularly concerned with how the next fellow was going to get through. Furthermore, a stiff wind was beginning to blow from the southwest, and dust and sand were beginning to fly.

I studied the map. It had an informative legend neatly boxed in red: *Roads in this area often impassable; tourists planning trips should make inquiries locally and carry water.* I threw the transmission into low range and headed in. It was slow, rough work and not much fun for a man with a sore back. The wind picked up as I went along, throwing sand and gravel rattling across the windshield. Every so often I had to pause for the visibility to improve enough so that I could see what hole which wheel was going to fall into next. At last I said to hell with it, pulled off into a jeep track, and drove over into the shelter of a tall reddish butte. It was only three o'clock but I was bushed; besides, it occurred to me that, considering all the circumstances, I had probably come far enough. I climbed in back, therefore, laid the rifle and shotgun on the floor, wrapped up in the blanket, and went to sleep.

It was dark when I awoke for no particular reason, feeling cold, hungry, cramped, and uneasy—mostly the latter. I picked up the shotgun as the better weapon for night operations, and broke it to check the loads. The twin brass heads of the shells gleamed dully in the darkness. I closed the piece again and got out of the car. The wind had not let up noticeably. The dust was still blowing along the ground but the sky was absolutely clear overhead. The stars were large and bright. The moon was rising in the east. Magnified and colored by the dusty atmosphere near the horizon, it looked orange and enormous. You've never seen a real moonrise until you've seen it on the desert; and when you do see one you won't believe it. There was something eerie about the wind rushing past under a cloudless sky.

I stood there for a while. Nothing moved within my range of vision, except the dust and a tumbleweed that, rolling past in the live and bouncing way they have, almost got the benefit of a twelve-gauge Magnum load of #2 shot. I walked around the car and stood on the other side for a while, gaining a great deal of respect for the old mountain men who lived with this kind of nagging uneasiness most of their lives, never knowing when death might be lying in wait for them out in the dark.

Finally I shrugged, opened the trunk of the car, unloaded the shotgun while standing clearly visible in the light from the trunk lid, and put the gun away in its case. Then I went back and got the rifle and did the same for that. Instinct told me I wasn't alone in this part of the desert; but it could have been the same kind of instinct that makes you hear noises in the kitchen at night when there's nobody but you in the house. And if Van Horn had put some men to following me, and they were hanging around out there, I certainly didn't want to shoot them; and if it was somebody else, I had driven five hundred miles to meet him, and I didn't want to shoot him, either—at least not yet. Of course there was the possibility that he might want to shoot me; but if I wasn't willing to take that chance I shouldn't have wasted my time and that of a lot of other people coming out here. I was gambling on the hunch that somebody had gone to more trouble to set this up than seemed necessary for a simple assassination. There was no sense in decoying me all this way just to kill me; it was a waste of effort. Whoever was running the show had something more elaborate in mind, I hoped.

I got the gasoline lantern and lighted it to make myself look guileless and unsuspicious; then I got the stove out and started it in the lee of the car with my cardboard carton of groceries for an additional windbreak. It was about nine-thirty. I put on water for coffee and fried up some bacon in the big iron skillet I carry—aluminum is fine for boiling, and I have a nesting set of the stuff, but give me iron for frying any day in the week. When it was done, I laid the bacon aside to drain on a paper towel, anchoring it well against the wind, and cracked three eggs into the grease in the skillet. I could remember Nina Rasmussen rustling up the same menu in the snowbound cabin some mornings ago; and I could clearly recall the last time I had done it myself outdoors like this, in the Jemez Mountains the first morning of deer season, an hour before I took a bullet in the back that almost finished me. It did not seem advisable to dwell on the thought.

Squatting there by the car in the bright white light of the lantern, I had plenty of time to think of other things too. I thought about Jack Bates, and about Larry and Ruth DeVry, and about my wife's scarf that had traveled, so Larry claimed, from the DeVry house to the lonely spot up in the mountains where Jack had been found dead. I should probably have mentioned that to Van Horn; however, it would have been only my word against that of the DeVrys should they decide to get together and deny it. But there was something very odd about the way the scarf had been left there by Jack's body, not casually to look as if it had been dropped by accident, not even tied in place as would have been easy enough to do without damaging the cloth, but, according to Van Horn's description, skewered brutally and obviously onto a dead limb by someone who, you could not help but think, must have hated its owner enough to take pleasure in feeling the thin silk tear; someone, you might say, who wasn't really planting a clue but simply affixing a label to the crime. . . .

Then the eggs were done and the water was hot enough for instant coffee—if I'd waited to boil the real stuff with that wind blowing I'd have been up all night—and I ate, cleaned up, and turned out the lantern. I picked it up by the bail as it flickered out, leaving me half-blinded by the sudden loss of light.

A voice behind me said harshly, "Just hold it right there, Dr. Gregory."

My hunting training kept me from jumping too far. "I'm holding it," I said. "Don't get nervous."

I heard footsteps moving closer. "Why didn't you come to Hanksville as you were told?"

I said, "A government man read your note. I figured he'd get to Hanksville ahead of me, having planes at his disposal. In fact, I suggested it. What else could I do?"

"He's there now."

"Okay, then," I said. "I thought you might be happier with another rendezvous, so I stopped off to give you a chance. I figured you'd be watching the road. The money's in the game pocket of my hunting coat, in back."

"Put the lantern down."

I did so.

"Back up," he said. I backed up slowly. He felt me for weapons in the customary places—hips and armpits especially—and did not find what he was looking for, since I had hidden it better than that. This time of year, with the amount of clothes I was wearing, it was no trouble. He reached into the big rear pocket of my coat and brought out a sample of the contents, examined it in the moonlight, and replaced it. At least I thought that was what he was doing; I didn't venture to turn my head to look. He sounded like a man under strain and I didn't want to worry him. I was under some strain myself. He spoke again. "Walk straight ahead. Don't try anything."

I walked straight ahead, following the butte around to the east. A jeep was parked there, looking black in the moonlight. As we approached it, another man came up from the right, carrying some kind of a rifle. I still did not know what kind of weapon the first man was pointing at me, if any; I was taking it on faith. They made a production of getting me into the vehicle. The second one covered me while the first one climbed into the rear, giving me a glimpse of the previously unseen gun—one of those small revolvers with the barrel sawed off at two inches. They both covered me while I got into the front seat. Finally the first man assumed the guard duty while the second got behind the wheel. Since I had no immediate plans for either escaping or attacking them, it seemed like a waste of effort. Then we drove for some miles across country. They used no lights and every little wash and arroyo looked like a black chasm across the moonlit plain. The wind was dying.

At last we entered what seemed to be the wide mouth of a canyon that narrowed rapidly to the west. There were sheer rock walls to the north and south. The wall to the south was in black shadow; the one to the north was silvery with moonlight. The driver turned the jeep on the level canyon floor and stopped it facing east. He turned on the lights once for about three seconds and turned them off again. We sat there without speaking for about ten minutes. At last he turned on the lights again and left them on. I heard the sound and saw the plane at the same time; it was almost on the ground before the lights picked it up. It taxied on by us.

The man behind me said, "All right. Out."

I got out. We walked over to the plane, which seemed to be making enough noise to be heard downwind clear to the Mississippi a thousand miles east. The pilot was on the ground.

He shouted over the racket: "A jeep's tracking you about two miles back. There's been an AEC plane running a survey over Monk's Canyon all day. What do you think they expect to find in those limestone strata?"

My escort said, "Can you lose them if they pick us up?"

The pilot laughed. "Those government boys wet their pants if they have to fly under a hundred feet. And at night, yet? Don't give it a thought."

The jeep was already driving away. We got in. The plane started to move. You could feel when it was airborne; I waited for the pilot to pull up for altitude, but he just kept boring straight up the canyon with the rock walls closing in from both sides. We weren't twenty feet off the ground. I thought the right wing-tip would touch when we banked for the first turn. Then the shadowed wall alternated with the moonlit one as we twisted and dodged up the narrowing gorge; a cliff loomed dead ahead and the pilot laughed and lifted us over it with, it seemed, only inches to spare, and dived for another canyon that opened up in front of us. This kind of horseplay went on for much longer than I care to remember. I don't even like rollercoasters, and they run on rails. It must have been a couple of hours. At last we hopped over a kind of a rim into pitch blackness beyond; suddenly two lights appeared ahead and below us. The plane changed course slightly to line them up and we dropped in to them. I saw the ground only an instant before the wheels touched. Then I was standing on the ground alone, happy to be there, and the plane was swinging around, taxiing, and taking off again.

"Better check to see if he's got a gun," somebody said behind me, and hands patted the conventional places for the second time that evening. The plane was a dim blot against the sky; the sound of it was almost gone. I didn't think I was going to miss it. I was standing in the middle of a kind of sagebrush flat in the floor of another canyon, the walls of which rose several hundred feet all around. Near by some people seemed to be sweeping the ground with brooms. It seemed like a silly occupation until I realized they were brushing out the tire marks of the plane. Another voice, a girl's voice, said, "Search him again, stupid. I know he's got a gun. I gave it to him."

I turned slowly around to face Nina Rasmussen.

TWENTY-TWO

SHE WAS HOLDING a kerosene lantern, so I could see her clearly. She was dressed as I had last seen her in the hospital at Espanola, in jeans and the big checked Mackinaw jacket. Her head was bare. The short, blonde hair, brushed back from her face, gave her a clipped and boyish look.

"Hi, Spanish," I said.

She held out her left hand. "Where's the gun, Jim?"

I studied her for a moment longer. Coming here, I had made allowances for several eventualities, in a theoretical sort of way; but that did not mean that I was fully prepared for this one.

"Excuse me while I turn my back," I said.

"Be careful, Jim," she said. "Even if you should manage to make a break, we'd catch you before you found a trail out of this valley. And even if you should find your way out and get away from us, you'd die of thirst out there before you reached a house or road."

I said, "Be your age, Spanish. I didn't come here to play hide and seek. I came to find my wife."

I turned away from her, unbuckled my belt, and reached inside my clothes for the cord that, tied to a light belt next to the skin, held the .22 pistol suspended down my leg. I had read that one in a book somewhere. The fellow who wrote the book probably never lived with the trick for any length of time; it had been damned uncomfortable. Even though it hadn't worked, they should give me credit for a good try. I fished the weapon out, untied it, and held it up and back of me. It was taken away. I disposed of the harness and dressed myself again. When I turned around, she had the gun tucked inside her own belt.

"Well," I said, "it shows you're never quite as smart as you think you are. I figured a bunch of amateurs might let that one slip by them."

Nina smiled. "Maybe that's why I gave you the gun. So we'd know what to look for when you got here."

I said, "Don't rub it in. Where do we go now?"

She looked around, and spoke sharply to the others: "Come on, let's get it cleaned up before a plane wanders over and sees the lights. Pull that dummy brush back on the landing strip. Hurry it up now!" She jerked her head at me. "This way."

Walking along beside her, I said: "You sound like a top sergeant."

"They need one," she said grimly. "Or a slave driver with a whip. They seem to think you can run an organization like this on nothing but fine ideals."

"Which brings up the point," I said. "An organization like what?"

"Haven't you guessed?"

I shook my head. "A fellow I know named Van Horn would like to blame it all on the communists, but I'm not so sure. I'll bet you're saving the world from something, but I haven't determined just what."

She laughed. "Well, you'll find out in the morning."

"What happens in the morning?"

"They hold a meeting and decide what to do with you. There's been some disagreement about policy lately, and you're to be the test case." She glanced at me. "Why don't you think we're communists, Jim? It seems like a logical explanation. You can blame anything on the communists these days, can't you?"

I said, "Personally, I give the Reds credit for a little more efficiency than this outfit's displayed so far. They're professionals; and this is an amateur production, judged by the sloppy way it operates. Professionals don't get so jumpy at the smell of blood. I've said that from the very beginning. This looks and acts like a collection of brilliant minds and weak stomachs; a lot of fancy ideas and no guts, Spanish."

She laughed again. "I think you're calling us names because I fooled you, Jim."

"You certainly did," I said bitterly. "I thought I was reasonably safe in trusting you. Not merely because you kissed me and gave me a gun to protect myself, but because I couldn't see you working with the gang that tried to kill your own brother. Maybe I should take back that remark about weak stomachs. Yours seems to be strong enough."

She hesitated. We were moving toward the canyon wall—the north wall, I decided, after a quick glance at the stars. I had lost my bearings completely in the air; I was not even sure we were still in the state of Utah.

"You have no right to say that," Nina said. "I went with you to save Tony's life, didn't I?"

"I wasn't accusing you of sending him to his death or even of knowing he was to be killed," I said. "Certainly when I pointed out the possibility, you were eager enough to go; and I'll admit you worked hard over him after we found him. But you know as well as I do who was responsible, and here you are associating with the very people who tried to murder him—in their usual fancy and gutless way. Van Horn and the authorities seem to think Jack Bates's death is tied in with the rest of this, but I don't believe it. The person who killed Jack had the nerve to stand in front of him with a gun and make sure of the job; and he didn't bother to dress up his work with a lot of clever trappings of accident or suicide."

She said, "You sound as if you judge a man's character by how well he commits murder!"

I said, "After all this elaborate pussyfooting around, a good, honest, straightforward murder is like a breath of fresh air. I can understand a person who hates somebody and grabs a gun and blows his head off. I can't understand this clever stuff. It's beyond me."

"Well, that's one way of looking at it. As for Tony—" She hesitated. "As for Tony, he died yesterday afternoon, Jim."

We walked a couple of steps in silence. "I'm sorry," I said. "I didn't know."

"They thought for a while they were going to save him. I think they told you so over the phone that morning. But he was just too weak, after the carbon monoxide. His heart couldn't quite make it, I guess." I did not say anything. She went on quietly, "Nevertheless, I'm here. Some things are bigger than mere personal relationships, Jim."

"Sure," I said. "Sure, Spanish."

"Just because . . . just because some fool got panicky for fear my brother was going to talk and sent somebody to kill him, does that mean I have to renounce everything I believe in? Besides—"

"Besides what?"

"Besides, I could be looking for the man who gave the order."

The swinging lantern in her hand cast the shifting, twisted shadows of the sagebrush out around us in every direction. Then we were climbing the talus slope at the foot of the cliff. We passed a building that seemed to be an old mine shack. Some fifty yards above it, we reached the shaft opening. The wooden shed protecting the mouth against slides from above looked battered and weatherbeaten, but it did not yet have the silvery patina of age that you find on some of the really ancient deserted structures scattered around that country. Inside, the tunnel was just high enough for me to walk erect. There was debris on the floor that had fallen from the roof. I don't like caves or tunnels or holes in the ground of any description.

"There is actually no mine called Ararat Three," Nina said behind me. "That happens to be our name for this place, and you weren't supposed to broadcast it."

"Why did you tell me then?" I asked.

"Because we wanted you to come looking for it. I was supposed to give you enough clues to start you in this direction; after all, it's the region people think of when somebody mentions uranium, isn't it? We were going to feed you more hints as you went along, until we had you out in the open where it was safe to move in and pick you up." She laughed. "You have quite a reputation as a dangerous man, Jim. Nobody was willing to tackle you alone. And then you messed up the plan by taking all kinds of people into your confidence. I don't quite understand that. I thought we could count on your working quietly by yourself; after all, your wife's still suspected of murder, isn't she?" I did not speak, and she went on, "Anyway, we had to take you out of circulation in a hurry, and the kidnap note seemed like the best bet although I admit it was a fairly corny idea."

"Well, it worked," I said. "I'm here."

"With a hide-out gun in your pants leg! Jim, I'm afraid you're kind of corny yourself. What were you planning to do, rescue your wife and fight your way clear with a smoking pistol?"

"Something like that," I said. "It would have worked, too, except for you."

She glanced at me, started to speak, and changed her mind. We were getting pretty far underground; I didn't like it at all. Nina spoke at last: "Actually, this place is known as the Big Judith Mine, but the local people call it Fleming's Folly. It seems that a rich easterner named Fleming was taken in by a very fancy salting operation, although the geologist told him you don't find uranium in this type of strata. Of course, Fleming knew better than to pay attention to them; if Steen and Pick had listened to the geologists, they wouldn't be riding around in Cadillacs now. So he bought this claim out in the middle of nowhere, and built miles and miles of road and put in heaven only knows how much expensive equipment—and of course all he ever got out of it was the truckload or so of high-grade ore that the swindlers had hauled in on muleback and planted artistically around for him to find. Anyway, that's the story that got around. When Fleming finally woke up to what had happened, they say he was so mad he just drove off and left all his equipment in here to rust. His road washed out the following spring, and a couple of slides helped to block it completely. Nowadays you can't even get a jeep in here, and not many people try. After all, it's been pretty well proved there's nothing here worth the trouble." She laughed. "Of course, Fleming was one of us, and his equipment was put to good use after he took his dramatic farewell of the place."

I said, "Pretty neat."

Nina said, "We have another entrance now, but you'd never find it without knowing where to look. We only use this one to meet the plane, since it can't land on the other side. It's about eight miles around to Number Two entrance by trail, and quite a climb, both up and down. It's only half a mile or so straight through."

I said, "Just between the two of us, I'd rather go around."

She laughed. "Does it give you the creeps? It did me, too, at first. It won't be so bad once we get below. Naturally we try to leave this part looking completely unused and deserted. There's always some optimist willing to go to a lot of trouble to poke around an old mine, even one that's supposed to be a dud."

A few rods farther on, the tunnel ended. Here a transverse passage explored the interior of the earth to right and left. We took the right-hand branch, moving only a dozen steps or so before the lantern light showed a mass of splintered timbers and fallen rock ahead. Before we reached this, Nina stopped and touched a switch or button of some kind, concealed in the right-hand wall. She waved me back a little. Part of the tunnel floor in front of us began to move, settling down and swinging aside heavily in the manner of a safe door or the breechblock of a naval gun. It left a round hole about three feet in diameter. Light streamed up through the hole and illuminated the roof of the passage. Nina raised the glass of her lantern and blew out the flame.

"Be careful going down," she said. "The ladder's kind of slippery."

I knelt and felt for the ladder with my foot, found it, and climbed down into a lighted chamber that disappointed me slightly. In the movies it would have had shiny plastic walls, tile floors, and indirect lighting. The people would have been wearing skintight leotards and little capes like Superman. I don't know why the costume of the future always has to look like a romantic variation on my winter underwear. But this was just another hole in the ground, a little more spacious than the passage I had just left, and much more heavily reinforced by timbering. The illumination was electric, to be sure; it consisted of an ordinary light bulb of about sixty watts in a dime-store porcelain pull-chain socket screwed to one of the timber uprights that lined the walls. Two insulated wires supplied it with current. I could have made a neater installation myself. Amateur handymen always mess up the heads of screws; while long experience with guns has made me finicky about using the right size screwdriver for a job. The place did have heat and ventilation; there was a definite movement of warm fresh air up through the open trapdoor.

The people awaiting us at the foot of the ladder were not dressed for outer space or the year two thousand; they were wearing jeans and overalls and the most noticeable thing about them was how dirty they were. Well, the area wasn't noted for the abundance of its water supply; but the woman, whom I did not know, could at least have combed her hair and put on lipstick, even though she was over fifty and fairly homely. The man, whom I did know, could have got hold of an electric razor somewhere, since they had juice down here, and shaved off the matted growth that masked the lower portion of his face. It took me a moment to recognize him. He had always been a very fastidious sort of person when I knew him at Los Alamos; fastidious and a little precious, and there had been rumors that certain facets of his sex life had been the subject of official investigation, but nothing had ever come of this, so forget I said it.

I said, "Hello, Louis," and held out my hand.

Louis Justin hesitated; then he took my hand and said, "Greg, I'm sorry about this. Believe me, it was none of my doing. If I'd known there was any thought of resorting to violence—"

He looked up, retrieved his hand, and used it to pull nervously at his beard, as Nina dropped down from the ladder near us. Louis looked self-conscious in his grimy jeans and denim shirt, although the condition of the garments indicated that he had worn them long enough to become accustomed to them.

He said, "Where are the others, Miss Rasmussen?"

"They'll be along in a minute, Doctor," Nina said. "Come on, Jim."

"Where are you taking him?" Louis asked.

"I have my instructions, Dr. Justin," she said.

"Oh. Well, all right."

We started down a sloping corridor sparsely illuminated by naked, dusty, forty-watts bulbs. I heard Nina laughing softly to herself.

"What's so funny?"

"All the bright little boys and girls," she said. Her voice had an edge of dislike. "That was Dr. Minna Goldman, the well-known microbiologist, in the overalls. All the bright little boys and girls waiting for the old world to go boom so they can jump out and start a new one."

"Is that what they're waiting for?"

"Certainly. What do you think this place is? It's an overgrown bomb shelter, complete with the latest defenses against radiation and fallout. Of course, the living conditions are a little crude, but you can't have everything."

I said, "Ararat. The mountain on which Noah landed his ark."

"Yes. Aren't we symbolical?"

I said, "Does the number 'three' also have mystic significance?"

"Such as?"

"Such as indicating the existence of Ararats One and Two, and maybe Four, Five, and Six?"

She laughed. "That comes under the heading of classified information," she said. We had stopped descending. She came to a halt at the beginning of what seemed to be a long, level, timbered hall. I could see doors and the openings of several transverse passages. Standing there, I was uncomfortably aware of all the tons of rock above me. The people who go crawling through caves for fun always amaze me; I can't even relax in the Chicago subway. Nina walked to a door on the right, knocked gently, opened it, and looked inside. Then she closed the door and glanced at her wrist watch. "I guess the Director's gone to his room," she said. "It's after midnight. Well, I'd better not disturb the old humbug. You'll meet him in the morning."

"I'm looking forward to it."

She turned to face me. "You've got nerve, Jim," she said after a moment. "Most of the people down here haven't. That's why they're here. Because they're scared. You might keep that in mind."

I said, "You're not scared, Spanish."

"No," she said, "and when you find out why I'm not scared you'll think even worse of me than you do now. Well, I'll take you to your wife."

I walked beside her down the hall. You could see the light bulbs down the timbered ceiling ahead in an interminable and not quite ruler-straight chain. An occasional one had burned out and not been replaced. We stopped in front of a door that, like the others, was rudely made of boards fastened to two crosspieces with nails that, longer than the double thickness of wood, had been turned and clinched. The latch was what you might expect on a garden gate; it was secured with a cheap padlock. They certainly hadn't wasted money on their fittings and hardware. Nina produced a key, unlocked and removed the padlock, and stepped aside.

"Jim," she said.

"Yes?"

"You were asking what these people are saving the world from. I'll tell you. They're saving it from people like you."

I looked at her for a moment. It was hardly the time to investigate riddles. I turned from her and went through the door, and heard her lock it behind me.

TWENTY-THREE

I HEARD SOMEONE stir in the darkness that was broken by a few rays of light leaking through cracks in the crude door behind me. They only made the darkness seem more intense. I heard the metallic, half-musical sound of bedsprings creaking. The low voice that spoke was completely familiar; I would have known it anywhere. Until I heard her voice I had not realized how much I had missed her.

"Greg?"

"Hi, Princess," I said. "Where the hell's the light switch around here?"

"Just reach in front of you; there's a chain. . . . Wait, I'll get it."

"I've got it," I said.

I pulled, and raw light flooded the place. It was a small room, or cave, about seven by seven by six and half under the beams; it looked even smaller because of all the timbering. It occurred to me that the mine above had not been reinforced in the rugged manner of these lower levels. I suppose they had built this part to stand up under shocks that miners do not usually have to consider in their calculations. It was logical enough in a nightmarish way; but it gave me the feeling that I was dealing with people who had withdrawn from reality into an elaborate sort of science fiction—or maybe I was the person who, with the best information in the world on the subject, was stubbornly refusing to face the truth about the probable fate of the earth.

The furnishings of the tiny chamber consisted of a folding chair, a wooden shelf bracketed to the wall uprights, and a narrow iron cot covered by an army blanket. A white receptacle of the type we used to have on the farm when I was quite young was tucked away under the cot. A towel, and the blue leather jacket she had worn away from our house in Albuquerque, hung from nails in the wall. The jacket had lost a great deal of its smart and jaunty look in the week or so since I had last seen it: it was scuffed and dusty.

She was sitting on the edge of the cot facing me. She was fully dressed. I don't know why it should have shocked me to find her still wearing the clothes she had departed in; after all, her suitcases had remained in Nevada with the wrecked sports car.

She said, "I'm sorry. I . . . just lay down to wait. I must have fallen asleep. . . ."

Her voice trailed away. She stood up. I had forgotten that she wasn't a very tall girl; or maybe I just neglected to make allowances for my cowboy boots. She looked up at me, pushing back a wisp of dark hair.

"You shouldn't have come," she said.

"Yeah," I said. "Sure. Just tell me and I'll go away."

We stood there looking at each other. Her face and hands and knees were clean, and her lipstick was bright and even; otherwise she was kind of a mess. Her dark hair was stringy, her shirt and shorts were wrinkled and grimy, her shoes were scratched and dusty, and there were holes in the heels of both her socks. Except for the clean face and the careful lipstick she looked like a tenement kid. She was the prettiest thing in the world. I had done some moderately crude and deceitful things to find her, and I hoped to do more to get her out of here; and she would be worth every lousy word and deed of it.

I said, "Princess, you look terrible. Who let you out in those pants?"

She said, "Darling, I saved up two days' washing-allowance to look this good for you, when they said you might be coming. And you might at least have the decency to get a shave before you start criticizing other people's appearance."

After a moment she reached up and ran her fingers across the stubble on my jaw; her hand hesitated, and suddenly her arms were around my neck and I was holding her tight—holding her, and kissing her, and holding her again as she cried. This did not last long; in a moment she lifted her wet face to be kissed again. We went into it more thoroughly this time, heedless of the bright lipstick that was getting well distributed over both of us. We were both aware when what had started as an affectionate reunion between two respectable married people began to turn into something considerably more violent and primitive. I felt her stiffen against me. She pushed away, and I let her go.

"Greg—"

I said, "I'm just getting rid of my hat and this damn big coat," I said, pulling them off and letting them fall.

"But there's something I have to tell—"

I caught her as she tried to back away, kissed her, and steered her backwards until the cot hit her in the back of the knees. She was trying to resist and to say something; but her resistance wasn't serious, and I continued to take care of her conversational efforts in the obvious way. I lowered her gently to the blanket. She tried to hold me off, but not as effectively as she might have. At last she twisted her face abruptly aside.

"Greg, there's something I've *got* to tell you. . . . Darling, stop that and listen!" She caught my wrists. "Don't, darling, you'll tear it and I haven't another damn thing to wear. Will you please, please *listen!*"

I said, "Princess, this is not the time to unburden your damn little soul. We can discuss your criminal career and what's to be done about it later. Right now we've got more important matters to attend to."

"But—" She looked up at me seriously; then she grinned, and put her arms around me, drawing me down. "It's not fair," she said rather breathlessly. "Well, just remember that I tried. And, Greg—"

"Yes?"

"Just because we're in a cave you don't have to act like a bear. The zipper's in back. . . ." A long time later, she whispered, "It's too bad there isn't a more dignified way of doing that. It might get to be quite a popular pastime."

I kissed her on the ear. I said, "Look who's talking about dignity with her clothes up around her neck."

"Darling, do you realize—"

"What?"

"Do you realize we didn't . . . do anything about it?"

"Do anything about what . . . Oh." I laughed. "Well, we'll worry about that nine months from now, if we're still alive."

"Greg, you shouldn't have come. I hoped you'd have sense enough not to come."

"Uh-huh," I said. "I noticed you disapproving vigorously just now."

"I know. I'm just a selfish bitch, darling. If . . . if I had any courage at all, none of this would have happened."

I said, "That's making you out awfully damn important."

"But it's true. At least I could have killed myself before I let them use me to trick you into coming here."

"That might have made you feel noble for a second or two before you kicked off, but it wouldn't have done me much good since I wouldn't have known about it." I sat up and got out my wallet. "Here's something you mislaid, Princess. Do you want it back? If you're planning to keep on commuting to Reno—assuming that we ever get out of here—I might as well hang onto it."

She looked at the ring, and studied my face; sat up, tossed back her hair and pulled her shirt down for a minimum of decency. She hesitated briefly, then held out her hand, and I slipped the ring onto the proper finger. She looked down at it, and rotated it between the thumb and forefinger of her right hand. Presently she spoke without looking up.

"Are you sure *you* want it this way, Greg? You haven't heard what I have to say."

I said, "Did you kill Jack Bates?"

"No, but—"

"Did you sleep with him?"

"No!"

"Did you ever obtain government information from me and sell or give it to communist agents?"

"Of course not!" she said indignantly.

"Then I can't see what the hell you can have done that's so terrible."

She played with the ring for a second or two before she spoke. "What if I'd lied to you?" she asked quietly at last. "From the very beginning, Greg. What if I'd let you believe—"

"Believe what?"

"Let you believe that we met by accident; that it was love at first sight; that I found you so irresistible and fascinating that . . . that I couldn't help but say yes when you asked me to marry you? What if all that was just a damn lie, darling? What if I was just acting under orders all that time?"

After a moment I got up from the cot, made myself a little more presentable, wiped the lipstick off my face, and picked up some garments off the floor. I turned and looked at her. She looked kind of cute, sitting there with not much more than a shirt on. I could not help reflecting that a

great many of the crises of married life can never be por-
trayed accurately on the stage or in the movies, because
the costumes of the principals generally wind up something
less than adequate. I tossed the stuff into her lap, after
glancing at it critically.

"You'd think all these great scientific minds could manage to promote enough water for doing a bit of laundry,"
I said.

"They've drilled a well," she said. "It goes I don't know
how many hundreds of feet down. Maybe thousands.
They're getting water but it all goes into the emergency
reserve tanks except just the minimum they can get by with.
Once they have enough stored, there'll be more to go
around. Don't tease me, Greg."

"I'm not teasing you. I'm just trying to think. My vanity
has suffered a terrible blow; I'm trying to bear up under
it." After a while, I said, "Whose orders, Princess? You
mean you belonged to this gang of sentimental nitwits?"

"Maybe I'm kind of a sentimental nitwit myself, Greg."

I said, "They sicked you on me, sent you to that cocktail
party with instructions to latch onto me if I floated within
range. . . . Is that right?" She nodded. I asked, "How far
did your instructions go? Was matrimony in the orders?"

She said, "It was left up to me. After all, they couldn't
very well come right out and order a girl to make such a
desperate sacrifice, could they, darling? Not even for the
good of humanity. But they were careful to impress on me
what a menace you were to everything we believed in—"

"And precisely what was that?"

"Why," she said, "peace, and freedom from this terrible
fear the whole world is living with these days, the fear of
complete annihilation."

"Sounds good," I said. "How long did you work for them
after we were married?"

"I never did, really. I couldn't. I mean, catching you was
fun. I felt clever and devilish; just a hell of a wicked and
fascinating woman. And then I woke up one morning and
there we were married and . . . and I loved you and I was
supposed to feed you sly questions with your breakfast coffee and sneak out to make my reports. . . . I couldn't
do it, darling. It wasn't just you, it was . . . well, everybody
in Albuquerque was taking security so seriously. Before, it
had just seemed like a bunch of silly rules. But suddenly
I realized that whether I liked it or not, it was the law and

. . . and I guess I just wasn't cut out to be a criminal, Greg. I'll break a speed limit, but that's as far as I'll go. I got in touch with them just once more, to tell them I was quitting. Of course, they wouldn't leave it at that; they kept sending various people to try to change my mind, including Jack Bates."

"Jack was one of them?"

"Only recently. I think he was leaving to come here when he was killed."

I asked, "How was your marrying me going to change the destiny of the world? How were they planning to use the information you got from me?"

"Why," she said, "they have to keep track of all the new developments—the new weapons. To make sure they build the proper safeguards into the shelters."

"That could possibly be the truth," I said, "but it could also be a gag dreamed up by somebody clever to get a bunch of fuzzy-minded idealists to do some espionage work in the sacred name of peace and humanity. It wouldn't be the first time that's happened. . . . There are more than one of these places?"

"Well, not right now. The first one, back east, became obsolete several years ago with the advent of the hydrogen bomb; it was too close to the big cities, anyway, and too small. They moved headquarters out here; but the second one was barely started when somebody discovered uranium within a few miles of it and the whole area was flooded with prospectors. So that one had to be abandoned. This is the only one in existence right now, as far as I know. Of course, more are planned. . . . People are scared, darling. They see something terrible coming; they feel that they have to do something . . . something to preserve at least a few remnants of the human race. . . ."

"So they crawl into a hole and pull it in after them," I said. "Well, that's one way of meeting the problem. But this outfit does a little more than dig holes in the ground. It operates with guns and knives, too. As I have good reason to know."

She met my eyes for the first time. "If you can believe I was aware of that, Greg, there isn't much use in our talking any more about it." She drew a long breath. "When I joined, it was simply an organization for people who believed that the world we know would be destroyed in a very short time by the stupidity of the politicians and the shortsightedness of the scientists who kept supplying them with ever more horrible and devastating weapons—scientists like you, Greg. We couldn't do anything to stop it—"

"Somebody seems to think he can. By murder."

"It was never even suggested when I was working with them three and four years ago," she said. "We took for granted we couldn't prevent the catastrophe; but we could provide places of refuge for a few selected people—"

"The new Noah's Ark," I said, "half a mile underground."

"Yes." After a moment, she said, "When I left you the first time, Greg, it was because I simply couldn't stand it any more; all the time watching to see if you suspected, waiting for Van Horn to stumble onto something, cringing whenever other married couples started talking about the romantic and accidental way *they* happened to meet. . . . I guess I wasn't much fun to have around; I was so jumpy and jittery, waiting for the ax to fall. Sometimes I even hated you for having been so blind. I tried to make myself tell you, but it wasn't just a matter of getting it off my chest. There was that damned security involved, and you'd have felt obliged to have me tell Van Horn, too; and maybe you'd have got into a lot of trouble because of me. I decided I'd better just get out before something like a baby came along to really complicate the situation."

She was silent for a second or two. Somebody walked down the corridor outside. The footsteps sounded hard and crisp against the solid rock floor. I was very much aware of being buried in the middle of a mountain. Natalie began to speak again.

"Then I heard you'd been hurt," she said, "and I just had to come back. Naturally, I wondered if it could possibly have something to do with this, but you were quite certain it was an accident, remember? And I knew I ought to leave you again, but I kept putting it off, telling myself I'd go the minute you were well. . . . And then Jack was killed, and my scarf was found there, and I didn't think it had anything at all to do with all of this, but I knew I'd never be able to explain without telling everything. And I knew that no matter what I said you'd insist on defending me even if it got you into trouble, no matter how you really felt about it, just because I was your wife. So I tried to get away so if they did arrest me it would be a long way off; besides, I didn't want to be there when you learned—" Her voice died away. At last she said, "Well, if there's anything I've overlooked in making a complete mess of everything, just let me know and I'll try to take care of it."

I said, "About that scarf: Larry DeVry seems to think Ruth put it there. He claims it dropped out of your coat while we were at their house the night Jack was killed."

Natalie looked up, a little surprised. "That's what I figured out, and that's why I think Jack's death hasn't anything to do with this. But what on earth made Larry confide in you?"

"It was hardly a confidence," I said. "There was some friction in the family. He was making like a jealous husband."

"Well, I guess he had reason, at least where Jack was concerned."

"Do you know that," I asked, "or are you just guessing?"

"Jack said so, and I don't know why he should have lied. He was getting tired of the whole thing. Men always feel very abused when a woman has the bad taste not to fall out of love precisely when they do."

I said, "If you knew where you'd lost the scarf, why the hell didn't you tell Van Horn when he sprung it on us?"

She shook her head. "Darling, I'd have been as good as accusing Ruth of murder, wouldn't I?" she said. "I'd have practically been saying that she'd killed Jack because he was leaving her, and tried to implicate me. And then I'd have had to explain why Ruth DeVry should be insanely jealous of me. . . . She must have seen Jack coming to our house; maybe she followed him some evening. He came over a few times while you were in the hospital. He used the excuse of bringing magazines for me to take up to you; actually he was trying to high-pressure me into coming back to work for the organization." Natalie glanced at me. "Ruth would give me a horse-laugh if she heard that; and I can't possibly prove it."

"Never mind Ruth," I said.

"Well, it's a little hard not to mind her," Natalie said. "She must have thought she was losing Jack to me. No woman's going to accept the fact that a man's just getting tired of her if she can possibly blame it on another woman; and Ruth always has hated me, because of you. And, don't you see, if I'd accused her of stealing my scarf, and if the police had broken her down and made her admit a lot of things, she'd undoubtedly have tried to justify herself by accusing me of stealing her lover. And I'd have had the pretty choice of letting that stand or explaining just why Jack had been coming around secretly to see me. . . ." She moved her shoulders jerkily. "Anything I said was bound to be wrong. I couldn't see anything to do but just get as far away as possible." After a moment she said, "Greg, what are you thinking?"

I said, "I'm thinking you're going to catch cold if you don't get some pants on." She got up and started to dress. I spoke to her back. "I came five hundred miles and let nervous characters wave guns at me and crazy men fly me around in airplanes. I was prepared to find a wife who'd committed murder and treason. I don't say I expected it, but it was certainly a possibility, and I was prepared for it. And I don't say I'd have helped her get away with it, but I'd certainly have strained the rules in her favor until they screamed for help. . . . After that, do you think I'm going to get worked up over the fact that you made a fool of me once, three years ago? Be your age, Princess."

"Oh, it isn't that," she said without looking around. "I wasn't afraid of . . . I knew you'd be nice about it. It's just that what I did makes . . . makes everything a lie that came after. Doesn't it? I mean, we just can't build anything on a start like that, darling. Can we?"

I said, "Maybe not. But we can always go back to the beginning and start over, Princess. In fact, I'd say we'd made a pretty good imitation of a new start already."

After a moment she turned quickly to look at me. I took a step forward, all that was necessary in that small room.

TWENTY-FOUR

THERE WAS, of course, no morning in the place any more than there was any other time of day. People just started to move around out in the hall. Natalie sat up beside me, yawned, and got up to turn on the light that we had turned off. We were both fully dressed; for one thing it had been cold with only the one thin blanket—although as another sign of dawn the ventilators were now blowing warmer air —and for another it had seemed more dignified to be ready if they should decide to come for us. We hadn't even tried to sleep; it had seemed like a waste of time. We had spent most of the time talking about things of no immediate importance.

Natalie tucked her shirt-tail in and stepped into her loafers, looked at me and laughed. "I can see I'm married to a real New Mexican. He doesn't even take his boots off to go to bed. If the government had sent us to Texas I suppose I'd have spurs to contend with." Her smile died. "Greg."

"Yes?"

"What are you going to do? You must have some plan."

"Not really," I said. "But stick as close as they'll let you and keep your eyes open. You might also carry your jacket instead of putting it on, just in case you see a logical person to throw it at. They'll be watching for tricks from me, but maybe not from you. . . . I haven't got a plan, Princess, but I've got a theory. With all due respect to your former friends, I can't help thinking they're a bunch of creampuffs. They haven't been able to commit a good straightforward murder so far; I'm gambling they aren't quite up to dealing with a man who doesn't mind getting a little blood on his hands. That may sound crude to you, but just remember it could turn out to be a pretty crude situation if something drastic isn't done. There's nothing more dangerous, in a clumsy and fumble-witted way, than a bunch of scared idealists. . . . And just one more thing, Princess."

"What?"

"Do you remember the girl who came to the hospital to shoot me some months ago? Nina Rasmussen?"

"I'd hardly forget her. Even if this place wasn't as full of gossip as an old ladies' home." Natalie smiled. "I know all about your little interlude in the woods, darling. What about Nina Rasmussen?"

"She's got a lot more stuff than most of these jerks; the ones I've met, at least. If I see a break coming, I've got to know that she's being taken care of. I'm leaving her to you. You took care of her once with a pitcher of flowers. There aren't any flowers around, but there are plenty of rocks. If things start to happen take her out of action even if you have to beat her brains out. Just watch yourself; she's got a gun."

Natalie hesitated, studying my face. "I thought—"

"What?"

"From what they said, I understood that you liked her."

"What the hell," I said, "has that got to do with it? I've got one wife; what do you want me to do, start a harem? There are times when you've got to stop loving the whole of humanity and concentrate on one or two specimens. Right now I'm working on getting you and me out of here, Princess. Nina Rasmussen may be a wonderful kid, but if she gets in the way, clobber her."

Natalie studied me for a moment longer; then there was a rattling sound at the door as somebody fitted a key into the lock, and she stepped forward quickly and kissed me hard on the mouth. "All right, darling," she breathed. "I'll clobber her."

I did not know any of the people who came in. They were really very considerate; first they took us to the washrooms and let us clean up, and then they escorted us into a small mess hall and fed us a breakfast that had the tastelessness of any kind of institutional food. There was only one cup of coffee because of the water rationing. As we were getting up, Nina came into the place. She needed combing and dusting-off; and somehow her tousled appearance did not seem quite as attractive to me as it once had. There's nothing like a good, passionate family reunion to enable you to regard other women with cold objectivity. The endocrinologists probably have an explanation for this phenomenon. Nevertheless, with her boyish stride, and the gun in her waistband and color in her cheeks, she made an interesting contrast to all the dreary, listless, underground faces we had seen.

"I'll take them to the Director," she said, and our escort melted away. Nina looked at me and smiled, and took the gun from her belt. She pulled out the clip and pocketed it, and drew back the slide to show me the chamber empty. "Just so you won't be tempted to grab for it and make a break, now that you have your wife back, Dr. Gregory," she said. "Big and brave as you are, I doubt that you could fight your way out of this place bare-handed. . . . Come on. They're waiting for you."

We walked down the hall together, and stopped at the last door, where we had paused the evening before. I felt Natalie take my arm and hold it tight. Nina knocked, received an answer, opened, and stepped back to let me pass. There were about a dozen people crowded into the small chamber we entered. I recognized Louis Justin and the woman Nina had identified as Minna Goldman, the microbiologist. Some of the other people looked vaguely familiar. The man behind the desk looked like a white-bearded prophet in overalls; for some reason I was reminded of John Brown of Kansas although the old abolitionist's hair and beard, in the painting I'm thinking of, are not white.

Nina said, "Here they are, Dr. Fischer."

I looked at the presiding figure again, watched him take off the rimless glasses he was wearing and polish them and replace them in a gesture that was out of keeping with the fierceness of his appearance—a gesture that was also very familiar. I had lived with that gesture for several months once, in Washington. Old Fischer always polished his glasses before tackling any new problem.

I said, "Long time no see, Paul. I should have known you were too stubborn to fall off a boat."

He looked at me steadily for a long moment. His eyes had developed a kind of blue impenetrability since I had last seen him; they seemed to be focused on nothing—or everything. You could not help wondering how the man could see out of them, when you could not see into them at all.

"Sit down," he said curtly, and we sat down on two of the folding chairs placed before the desk. Natalie arranged the blue jacket neatly across her knees. I noticed that Nina had not come into the room with us. The door was closed and Fischer looked over our heads at the others, seated and standing.

He began to speak abruptly. "There have been some protests against the policies of the governing councils since I took office eight months ago. It seems that certain members of our organization feel that we are pursuing too aggressive a course; that it is our duty to wait passively for annihilation without raising a hand against those who, usurping the powers that are God's alone, would turn them loose to destroy all mankind. To make the issue clear, I've had such a man brought here. Some of us have worked with him; I myself have remonstrated with him, to no avail. I don't say he is evil and deserves to die; such judgments belong to God. I merely say that if he continues to live he will continue to put thousands—perhaps millions—of other lives in danger. I can't see that we have any choice but to remove him. The woman, having once been one of us, and having deliberately chosen to transfer her loyalty to this man, deserves no consideration."

He stopped talking. After a while there was a stir behind us, and Louis Justin's voice asked, "You mean we should kill them? But that's murder!"

A woman's voice said, "I did not leave my home and work to become a member of a gang of assassins!"

Fischer smiled and spread his hands. "Very well then. If that's the consensus of the group, I suggest that you give these two people some provisions and show them the way out of here—unless you think we should radio the plane and send them back to civilization in style. They can tell their story to the police faster that way."

There was a moment of silence; then Justin's voice said angrily, "It seems to me, Dr. Fischer, that you could have asked for our opinion *before* you brought them here and put us all at their mercy!"

"That's just the point," Fischer said calmly. "I had Dr. Gregory brought here, regardless of what he might learn about this place, for the simple reason that we are all at his mercy anyway, or soon will be if he is allowed to continue with his work. You have all read Dr. Bates's last report concerning the recent disastrous government test in Nevada, but even though some of you were involved in the research leading up to it, as I was, you don't seem to have caught the full significance of it. That test, ladies and gentlemen, presages a weapon that will make this place as

obsolete as the weapon tested at Bikini made our first refuge. And even if it does not live up to its evil promise,
it's only a matter of time before some other weapon does.
If these men who put themselves above God and humanity
are allowed to continue their reckless probing into the for-
bidden secrets of the universe, our best efforts at finding
sanctuary are bound to meet defeat. Our choice is plain:
either we give up our purpose altogether, or we strike back
before it is too late."

Nobody spoke. After a while, Fisher went on: "You'll
want to know a few practical matters, how we can dispose
of these people in such a way as to divert attention from
this place. Dr. Gregory is known to have been looking for
a mine called Ararat Three; he will be shown to have found
such a mine—we have located a suitable old digging in the
desolate country to the north, and preliminary work has
been done to make it look convincing as a hide-out. There's
already some doubt about Dr. Gregory's loyalty; he has
been suspended from his government position. We are prepared to leave clues to indicate that he joined his wife at
the false Ararat Three and fled with her out of the country,
the escape financed by money obtained from his father-in-
law on the strength of a forged kidnap note, money which
he is carrying in his coat at this moment. Of course, this
plan entails insuring the complete disappearance and per-
manent silence of the couple, but there are many old mine
shafts on the desert, and I won't bother your consciences
with the actual details. All I want, since this is a democratic organization, is your assent to this step." He paused,
and threw out his arm dramatically. "Don't look at me.
There's your problem! Either let them walk out of here with
what they know, and give up all our hopes and plans, or
kill them! You have no other choice."

I waited until his arm came down; then I said, "Do I
get to say something?"

He hesitated. There was a murmur from the room, and
he said quickly, "Of course. If you have anything to say,
I'm sure we'll be interested in hearing it."

I got up cautiously. In that place I was never quite sure
that one of the rafters wasn't going to catch me an undig-
nified crack on the head. I turned to face the room, and
said, "I've only got two things to say. First, as Dr. Fischer
indicated, this shelter is already on the verge of being obsolete; and whether I get back to finish my work or not

doesn't matter. Somebody'll take over where I left off. Maybe the world isn't ready for that particular toy, but it's here and you'd better learn to live with it." I looked down at Natalie, whose face was turned up to me, and spoke to her: "As for the right and wrong of what I'm doing, or a thousand other men are doing in a thousand laboratories in this country and others—all I'll say is this: nobody's ever managed to turn the clock back yet. They haven't even managed to stop it. Do you want to stop it? Would you like our knowledge to stay in this incomplete and half-digested state forever? So far there are still people who think they can arrange a war in such a way as to destroy a lot of other people but not themselves. Whether they are right or wrong doesn't matter; what matters is that they may try. Should we leave it at that? Or should we go on to the point, not so far away, where every citizen of every nation will *know* that when a certain button is pushed, by anybody at all, right or wrong, the world ends; and that therefore they'd damn well better see that it doesn't get pushed. I'm working on the assumption that the quicker we get to that point, the better; and so are a lot of other men I know. Maybe there'll still be somebody crazy enough to commit suicide for the whole human race after we're finished; but in that case there's no hope for us anyway. I'd rather think that when people know enough, they'll figure out a way to live in peace, if only because they have to."

It was probably the longest non-technical speech I had ever made in my life. I'll never know how it went over, because just as I was sitting down there was a jolting jar that seemed to shake the whole place, and the lights went out. They came on again immediately as some kind of emergency equipment took over from the main generators—you could tell the difference; this current was weak and uneven. In the yellow, flickering light I could see the room filling up with dust shaken from the ceiling. Little rivulets of dirt were trickling down from between the heavy beams. I felt Natalie close by and put an arm around her. Out in the hall somebody shouted:

"Fire! Fire at Gate Two. The north tunnel is on fire!"

The room began to empty. I heard Fischer's voice barking orders. I made my way with Natalie toward the wall and squeezed us in between two of the upright timbers. A man came rushing in and made a report; the fire was gaining, they were running short of water, he needed the key to Number Four Tank. Justin caught him as he was running out with it.

"What started it, man?"

"I don't know. An explosion of some kind. We haven't been able to get in far enough to see."

"Is the north entrance open?"

"Can't tell. She's burning pretty damn hot; those timbers are really dry."

"What about the south entrance?"

"No trouble there as far as I know, Doctor."

The man started out again, stopped, and backed up. In the doorway stood a thin man who held some kind of a diminutive machine gun. I'm not up on military weapons, but the thing was short and light, and the hole in the barrel was somewhere between 6 millimeters and .30 caliber. The piece had a long magazine that I estimated would hold at least twenty rounds; maybe more if the cartridge was small. The man himself was no creampuff. He was dark, with wide cheekbones and deep-set eyes that had a glow in them that went with the gun. I knew that he enjoyed holding it and wanted to use it. I'd had the feeling myself, although never with respect to human beings. There was somebody behind him.

He moved forward with the shuffling gait of a man who wants to be sure of his footing; and Nina Rasmussen stepped into the room with her slim-barreled pistol in her hand. I did not have to look at the gun to know that the clip was no longer in her pocket. I could tell by her face.

TWENTY-FIVE

THE VENTILATORS HAD picked up some smoke now and were distributing it throughout the place. What with the dust and the smell of smoke and the knowledge that we were buried—and might be trapped—far underground, the guns seemed almost like a minor threat. There was a distant sound of shouting and excitement from down the corridor, but in our neighborhood everything was very quiet. The man with the submachine gun was covering the little group consisting of Dr. Fischer, Justin, the Goodman woman, and the man who had come for the key to the water tank. Nina located Natalie and me and signaled us forward with the barrel of her pistol.

I said softly, "Careful now, Princess. We won't try anything unless it looks good. If the lights go out again, stick close."

"Dr. Gregory!" Nina said sharply.

I moved away from the wall and went to her, stopping when the gun steadied warningly. She looked at both of us. I did not think she liked my arm across Natalie's shoulders, but I left it there anyway.

She said, "We're taking a trip, Dr. Gregory. There are some people who'd like to see you and ask you a few technical questions. Not that they need your help, you understand; but there are a few aspects of your research that are not fully understood where we are going. I'm sure you'll be glad to co-operate—particularly since your wife's continued health and welfare will largely depend on your attitude."

I looked at her face. Her eyes were very bright and she looked quite handsome despite the heavy clothes and a smear of dust along the temple.

I asked, "How many people are you working for, Spanish?"

"All the people in the world," she said. "And some day they'll realize it, and remember those who saved them from tyranny and exploitation."

I said, "That's a lot of bunk and you know it."

"Maybe I do. Maybe I'm just smart enough to get on the side I expect to win. It doesn't matter very much, does it? Martinez!"

The dark man spoke without turning his head. "Señorita?"

"Watch these two, the man in particular. He thinks he is big and tough, understand?"

"*Sí*. I understand."

The short machine gun swung toward us. Nina looked at me for a moment longer; then turned aside and walked over to the other group with the pistol dangling loosely in her hand. Dr. Fischer drew himself up as she approached.

"Miss Rasmussen," he said, "what—"

"You old maniac," she said softly. "You took to killing very nicely, didn't you? All it needed was somebody to convince you of the logical necessity—and you didn't take much convincing, as I remember. But it wasn't enough to send a bunch of eager kids out to slaughter people who didn't agree with you, for the sake of the human race. No, you had to start thinking of yourself as all-wise and all-powerful with the right to judge and to punish . . . ! What had Tony done that he deserved to die?" she cried. "What gave you the right to have him killed? You old fool, did you really believe you had divine guidance? I'll tell you whose guidance you had: mine! And I assure you I didn't get my instructions from above. . . . No, stand back!"

She lifted her gun with an easy movement. Dr. Fischer paused and looked at the weapon with that curious, detached, unfocused stare of his. Then he started moving toward it deliberately. There was no expression on his bearded face. She shot him accurately through the middle of the forehead. The report of the small caliber cartridge was loud and sharp in the confined space. The gun hardly jumped at all; and Dr. Fischer was not jolted in any way by the impact of the bullet. He merely died and fell to the floor in a kind of loose continuation of the step he had been taking when the gun went off.

The girl looked down at him for a moment. Then she turned abruptly to cover the three others, but they had not moved. She turned with the gun raised, poised in her hand with her finger off the trigger, the way you carry a gun that is loaded and cocked anywhere but in the movies.

"All right," she said. "Let's go."

We went out of the office. In the hall outside, the smell of smoke was stronger. The man called Martinez stopped at the foot of the sloping tunnel that led upward to the hatch through which I had been brought the previous evening. Natalie and I went ahead with Nina following. Presently we felt the jar of a single shot behind us. Later, as we continued to climb, we felt two more. There was no one in the chamber below the hatch; and the hatch was open.

"We'll wait for Martinez," Nina said, and we stood there awkwardly under the opening, waiting. She stood a little apart from us, very alert since she was alone. I could feel the air flowing past, laden with smoke. I tried not to look too eagerly at the hole in the ceiling that led out of this place. "I have some good news for you, Mrs. Gregory," Nina said abruptly. "It came in over the radio early this morning. You'll be glad to know you're no longer under suspicion of murder. Dr. DeVry gave himself up for the killing of Dr. Bates late last night."

Natalie started. "*Doctor* DeVry!"

"Does it surprise you? It's not the first time a husband has killed his wife's lover."

"But—" Natalie glanced at me, bewildered. "He must be trying to protect Ruth."

I said, "The way they were acting last time I saw them, it doesn't seem likely." I thought for a moment, and grimaced. "Princess, does it occur to you that Larry's the kind of guy who never looks at what his wife or any other woman's wearing?"

"What do you mean?"

"I mean if he was going out of the house, and saw a scarf on the closet floor, what would he naturally think? That it was Ruth's, of course! Larry took the scarf up there and hung it in the tree after shooting Jack, because he wanted everybody to know why he had done it. He was justifying himself and accusing his wife of adultery—only the scarf turned out to be yours. And when he found Ruth with me the other night and started talking about the scarf vaguely and menacingly, he wasn't accusing her at all; he was actually hinting that it was he who had killed Jack and if I didn't lay off I'd get a dose of the same medicine. . . ."

There was the sound of running footsteps from the tunnel. Nina stepped back, holding her little gun ready. Martinez came trotting into sight, and she relaxed. The man came up to us, and stood guard while she climbed the ladder. Natalie went up next and I followed; and Nina held her gun on us while Martinez climbed up to join us, hampered by his weapon.

"We'll go ahead while you set the charges," Nina said to him as he stood up. "Give yourself plenty of time with the fuses. We'll wait for you outside."

"*Sí, señorita.*"

The walk to the mouth of the shaft did not seem as long as it had the evening before; the first trip always seems the longest. Suddenly the opening was before us. Sunlight had never looked so good. We stood in the mouth blinking at the brightness outside. It was like waking up from a bad dream, even with the girl and her ready gun behind us. The sky was blue and without a cloud. Even the barren scenery was beautiful. I had not seen the place before in daylight. It was a deep valley with precipitous sides and a flat floor, in the center of which a small plane was waiting. The propeller was turning over so slowly that you could almost, but not quite, see the shape of it. A man leaned against the fuselage, smoking a cigarette.

Nina urged us a little way down the hill to one side and stopped to wait. She said, "We'll fly down into Arizona and wait for darkness before crossing into Mexico. I don't know the plan beyond that; but there are several routes to choose from. Don't waste time hoping for rescue. Your friend Van Horn may trace you this far—in fact we intend that he shall—but he'll think you're still underground. The north entrance is already blocked by tons of rock, and Martinez is taking care of this one. Even if your friends bring enough equipment to dig their way back in, they won't find anybody alive who saw you leave; and they'll never be able to prove that you aren't in there somewhere, buried in the debris or burned unidentifiably. So they won't be looking for you very hard elsewhere."

Natalie looked at her and shuddered slightly. "You're going to bury them alive, all of them? Just to cover your trail?"

"Were they ever alive, Mrs. Gregory?" Nina smiled. "They had already withdrawn from the world into their own little sanctuary. Let them stay there."

Natalie stared at her for a moment longer, and looked at the tunnel mouth behind us. Suddenly she buried her face in her hands. I put my arm around her.

"Sit down, Princess, and take a load off your indignation," I said. "Nobody in there's any great loss and you know it."

She let herself be led aside, and sat down on a rock. I sat down beside her and scratched my right leg through the damn cowboy boot that was beginning to throw all the muscles and bones of my foot and ankle out of their proper alignment. After all, I'd been wearing the things constantly for almost two days.

I said, "Personally, I don't give a damn what happens to them. They're all a bunch of screwballs as far as I'm concerned."

"They're people, aren't they?" Natalie said without looking at me. "Whether they've been right or wrong, they don't deserve—"

The ground shook, and dust welled out of the mouth of the shaft. Through it, Martinez came running, followed by a louder, closer blast, and a third, still closer. Martinez came sliding down the slope with his machine gun. He looked at Nina and bared his teeth in something that might have been a grin. A fourth blast sent rocks flying out of the mouth of the tunnel and rolling down the slope. Then there was silence as the dust settled.

"I can't stand it!" Natalie cried suddenly, starting to her feet. "We've got to do something—"

I saw the blue leather jacket fly through the air straight into the dark face of Martinez, who had jumped to intercept her. In the same instant I had the hunting knife out of its sheath in my boot; and I swung it like a scythe at the jean-clad leg of the girl who stood above me. She tried to step aside, but the edge sliced wickedly through cloth and flesh and grated on bone; she screamed and lurched back and lost her footing among the loose stones. I struck at the .22 pistol as it flailed wildly through the air—a backhand blow with my left hand that sent the weapon flying.

"Take her, Princess!" I cried. "Keep her away from the gun!"

I was aware of Natalie throwing herself onto the fallen girl who was already scrambling after her lost pistol. But I had no time to help; Martinez had fought his way free of the coat that had briefly blinded him, and the short barrel of the machine gun was swinging in my direction. I caught it with my left hand and shoved it aside and stepped inside it; Martinez grabbed for my right wrist and missed; and the knife went home to the hilt. I felt him stiffen convulsively under the shock; the gun came free in my hand. I stepped back, taking gun and knife both with me, and watched him fall. He was clawing for something under his coat; maybe the place that hurt, maybe another gun. I had no time to take chances with him; I rammed the butt of his own weapon down hard across his neck, and swung to help Natalie. She wasn't there.

Neither of the girls was there, and the .22 pistol was gone, also. Then they rolled into sight far down the talus slope, the weapon waving above them. I started down after them, keeping an eye out for the man who had been by the plane. He stuck his head out from behind a clump of sagebrush and aimed a revolver at me. The range was about a hundred yards, long range for a hand gun, but I fell flat anyway and looked at the weapon I had taken from Martinez. The safety was easy enough to figure out. There was another lever that probably switched the thing to full automatic, but I didn't monkey with that. I heard the sound of the shot during this research. The bullet struck some distance above me. I shoved the knife into my boot, got the butt of the machine gun to my shoulder, lined up the sights at the bush, and pulled the trigger. The recoil wasn't much but the muzzle blast, from that short barrel, was considerable. The empty cartridge tinkled on the rocks to my right. I squeezed off again, and again, pecking at the bush. On the fourth shot, out he came, running for the plane. It was an easy, straightaway shot. I held it a little higher for the increasing range and brought him down.

I got up and looked down the hill toward the mine shack near which the girls had been struggling. There was nobody in sight. I started running, and stopped, as a small scarecrow figure came around the side of the structure, leaned against it for a minute, and went to hands and knees; then fought its way up again and came stumbling toward me. I was with her in an instant, sliding and skating down the loose debris of the slope to reach her. She fell against me, sobbing for breath. I held her off to look at her. She had lost both shoes, most of her shirt, and about thirty per cent of her shorts; she was covered with dirt and blood. I pushed the tangled hair back from her face.

"Princess, are you all right? Are you hurt?"

"It . . . went off!" she gasped.

"The gun?"

She nodded, and buried her face in my coat, holding me tightly.

"Did it. . . . Are you *hurt,* damn it?" I cried.

She shook her head.

"Okay, then," I said. "Okay. Why didn't you say so in the first place?" I took my handkerchief and started to wipe the stuff off her face, but changed my mind and kissed her hard instead. "Don't scare me like that, Princess! Here, let me look at those knees. Damned if you don't look like you'd been through the meat grinder—"

"You'd better go to her, Greg. I think she's dying."

"Let her die," I said. "To hell with her."

"You don't mean that."

"No," I said. "I guess not. But you stay here. Take my coat, maybe fifty thousand bucks will keep you warm." I got out of it and put it around her and kissed her on top of the head. Then I picked up Martinez's gun and went down there, swinging wide and turning the corner cautiously. Nina was lying just behind the shack, her knees drawn up and her arms hugged tightly to her chest. I saw the .22 pistol gleaming among the loose stones near by. I moved up carefully and picked it up; then I knelt beside her.

"Jim?" she whispered.

"Uh-huh."

She turned her head slowly to look up at me. "You had a knife," she said reproachfully.

"Uh-huh. I had a knife. A gun *and* a knife. So that smart little girls who got the gun would think they had it all."

"You suspected—"

"Not really. I was just ready, if it should turn out that way. After all, you'd shot at me once. You'd taken me for a walk once and your brother was waiting when I got back to the car. You were cute as a little round button, but I remember when people try to kill me. I told you that once. Is there anything I can do for you?"

"No." After a while, she said, "Yes. Call—" She fought for breath. "Call me Spanish once more, Jim."

"Hi, Spanish."

"We would have made a good team, on the same side."

"I'd never be on your side, Spanish."

"That's stupid. We're going to win. Not here, not now; you had a little luck; but in the long run nothing can stand against . . . against . . . nothing. . . ."

She was dying. I couldn't argue with her. "Sure, Spanish," I said. "Sure."

She did not answer. After a while I stood up and looked around. There was a lot of work to be done. We'd have to get help in here somehow with equipment to dig through the blocked tunnels. It should not be necessary to walk out. Van Horn would have searchers out all over this country. But if the plane down there had a radio we might hurry them up a little; otherwise a smoke signal might help. The shack should burn nicely. I looked down briefly; then I went up the slope to my wife, who was waiting.